A Nebraska Apocalypse Novel

FELICIA JEDLICKA

To those who have endured less than perfect and still read on.

More titles by FELICIA JEDLICKA

DESTINY REJECTED
DESTINY RECLAIMED
DESTINY RAZED
DESTINY RESTORED

DÉJÀ VU

SAVE THE HUMANS

THE NECROMANCER'S CHILD

SISTER WITCHES
THE DEVIL'S SHADOW
THE DEVIL'S SOUL

THE NEBRASKA APOCALYPSE NOVELS
CORN COWS AND THE APOCALYPSE
COW TIPPING AFTER THE APOCALYPSE
CORN HUSKING AFTER THE APOCALYPSE

THE WARDEN SERIES
SUCCESSORS
RIVALS
LOVERS AND LIARS
BAD BLOOD
TENANTS AND TYRANTS
THE RING BEARER
GODS AND MONSTERS
BEASTS AND BURDENS
MAGIC AND MAYHEM
FORK IN THE ROAD
DETAILS AND DEADLINES

Cow
Tipping
The After
Apocalypse

Prologue

"T his is Jimmy the Card reporting way too damn early in the morning. It's a solemn day here in the Big O. For those of you not able to make it to last night's tournaments, you missed a hell of a show and a damned shame of a finale. One of the entrants, August Smith, was sadly stabbed to death by a grim during the last round of her sword competition.

"Mayor Thompson has extended his condolences to the friends and family of August as they mourn her loss. He reports that although her death is tragic, he will not stop the competitions. He says accidents are a part of any sport, and this one incident should not be used as an excuse to shut down an event that has provided much-needed entertainment during these trying times.

"The Mayor said he will strive to make the necessary changes to ensure the safety of future participants and he hopes the people of the metro will rally against the true adversaries of this crime, the grim.

"While the mayor tries to incite a mob mentality, *I* will be the voice of reason. The tournaments, albeit exciting, are not to be taken on by the faint-of-heart or the weak-of-spirit. We've been having fun with the decimation of the grim so far, but once again, people, this is not the zombie apocalypse. This is the motherfucking reckoning. If you want to step into the ring with a bumbling brain-hungry corpse, then you'd better go to comic con. If you want to take on the grim, then you'd better be strong enough to stare into the face of evil and not piss yourself."

Ashes to Ashes

ESPITE WHAT I WANTED, there was no retribution to be taken for August's death. Just as I suspected, the mayor used the incident to incite further rage against the grim. I knew Adrian Dorn had plotted to kill August. However, without proof, I would have only announced my intentions to be his enemy, so I kept my mouth shut. In the end, the tragic *accident* was no more newsworthy than an auto collision.

We brought August's body back to a cemetery not far from Priest's burned-down church. Garrett and Devin dug a hole, painstakingly slow, through the semi-frozen soil. I was envious they had the manual labor to alleviate the stress of their grief.

Haden stood with me by the body. She was keeping herself under control, but I knew her red nose wasn't from the cold. I didn't know how to handle the anger they were all harboring for me, but I knew one on one was probably the best way.

"Haden," I started.

"Don't," she said before I could even formulate my next words. "Don't apologize. I can't stand to hear you say that right now."

"I wasn't going to. I have nothing to apologize for," I lied. "I didn't kill August."

Haden glared at me. This wasn't the best approach, but it was direct and I wasn't going to spend months begging for forgiveness. I loved August, and I was willing to die for her. Just because I didn't succeed in doing that, didn't mean I wasn't trying. "You were supposed to be her savior. That's what all of this was about. She trusted you with her life."

I took in those statements and wondered if Haden didn't fully understand their meaning. "I couldn't have stopped them, you know that, right? I could have been there five seconds earlier, but there was still three of them."

"I could have," she snarled.

"Yes, you could have." My admission surprised her. She looked me over to see if I was sucking up or admitting my own failings. "Why do you think they made you the focal point of the day—the photos, the interviews. Haden, Adrian Dorn played us like a fiddle. He distracted you." Her jaw dropped open as she started to understand where everything had gone wrong.

"It was a setup?" She winced, letting a few tears show that she probably would have preferred to hide. "Why? Why August?"

"I don't know. Maybe because she saw right through his mask the second she saw him. Dorn's number one on my bad guy list right now, but I can't go after him until I have more information. I want to know what his cards are. I assume he didn't like the idea of the three of you in the finale together, but I'm just grasping at straws."

"How did you figure it out?"

"They were doing too good of a job blocking Garrett. He would have been close enough to help her. You were preoccupied." Her eyes sunk at the observation. "Devin was distracted by the girly dancers.

I saw Adrian nod up to the light guy. I went on instinct after that. I didn't even know the grim were armed until I was a few feet away.

"I thought it was only the two, but... it wasn't. I tried, Haden. I really did. I followed my instincts, and it still wasn't enough. All I got for my effort was sixteen more seconds than I would have had I stayed in the stands."

Haden looked down at the black body bag the medical staff had put August's body into for the trip back. She was silent for a long moment. When she looked back at me, her face was hard, as if she had secured her anger to avoid appearing weak. "What did she say to you?"

I shook my head. I didn't want to tell Haden that August asked me to lead the team. Whether Haden and I had a good relationship was debatable, but if I told her she was going to be following my instruction from here on out, there might not even be a debate.

"Be strong, don't give up." I chuckled, feeling my own tears return. "The usual cache of August's pep talks."

"I envy that. I should have hopped out of the stands the minute I saw you running across the field. I should have—"

"Don't do that to yourself. I've gone through a thousand what ifs, and none of them change this." I glanced down. "She loved you. She was proud of you. One more time hearing it wouldn't change how much this hurts."

Haden sucked in a deep breath as my statement broke her resolve to stay calm. She sputtered uncontrollably, and partly against her will, I hugged her. She eventually stilled and let me hold her while she wept. I knew for the time being it was all the comfort I could offer, but I was glad she let me offer it.

Dirt to Dirt

FTER THE SOIL WAS packed tight, we took turns offering a private statement to August's final resting place. I took my turn last while everyone milled about outside the fence trying not to show how much they were really hurting. I knelt down next to her grave and turned so they couldn't see me.

I said a short prayer that wasn't from any standardized religious text, but something that felt right. I didn't know if He still listened to any of us anymore, but I simply reminded Him that August was one of the good guys.

When I finally got up, everyone had convened to stare out at the road. An SUV was making its way down the gravel toward us, leaving a plume of dust in its wake. Haden immediately pulled her gun and ducked behind the Dodge. Garrett's sword was still lashed to his back, but he didn't reach for it. He and Devin strolled down the driveway like a sheriff and his deputy ready to acquaint any newcomer with a summary of the law.

I stepped through the cemetery gate as the behemoth black Tahoe pulled up. With the engine still running, our guest stepped out of the vehicle. At first, I only saw his boots—steel-toed, if I had to guess. His jeans, despite being boot cut, had extra rips to fit over the thick work boots.

Indifferent to the cold, he wore a t-shirt with a long-sleeved gray button-up shirt. The outfit was too young for him, but he probably hadn't given much thought to style over the last decade. He was at least clean-shaven and his dark waves, which looked perpetually greased, were trimmed short and pushed back out of his eyes... mostly.

I stumbled, but recovered as I walked over. I could hardly keep myself upright with this new development on top of the last twenty-four hours. Haden holstered her gun. Devin and Garrett parted to let me by. I was glad no one said anything to me about him. One word about him being an inappropriate friend would have sent me reeling into the realm of scary mad.

Priest removed his sunglasses and gave me the most sympathetic look anyone had offered me thus far. Everyone was still immersed in their pain and trying to figure out who to blame for August's death. At present, I was the winner; therefore, I had no one to lean on. Until now.

I stopped in front of him, looking him over. His eyes were bright, awake, and sober. The shakes were gone, and more importantly, he wasn't burnt to a crisp like I thought he had been.

"You're alive," I whispered.

His eyes widened and his brow dipped in confusion. He was about to speak, but that's when I hit him.

Hard Knocks

I WOULD LIKE TO say I offered him a lady-like derisive slap, but my intent was not to discipline him for errant behavior. My intent was to hurt him, like his supposed death hurt me. Up until then, I hadn't realized how much I had missed him. Seeing him reminded me that I should have mourned him, but didn't, because I was selfishly engrossed in trying to keep my team from abandoning me.

My fist grazed his cheekbone in a solid backhand. It wasn't enough to give him a black eye, but it would make it uncomfortable for him to chew for a while. He cradled his face and stared back at me in shock. I wanted to hit him again, and I even stepped forward to do so, but Garrett and Devin pulled me back.

Priest and I were locked in a silent battle. My eyes were starting to water, and his were returning to their former expression of sympathy. I sniffled, trying to decide if I was crying for him, for August, or for everyone who hated me right now.

I didn't care if I was supposed to be a strong leader. I just wanted people to stop leaving me. My resolve broke and let my body go slack. I was prepared to drop to the ground and freeze my face to the snow with my tears, but Devin hoisted me up into his arms.

There was a short discussion before Devin slipped into the back of the SUV with me still cradled on his lap. I felt ridiculous, but I couldn't stop crying and I didn't foresee a future where I would be able to stop.

There There

I VAGUELY REMEMBER DEVIN shoving something in my mouth, handing me water and telling me to drink. After that, I was out like a light. When I finally woke up, the house was quiet: no radio, no television, and no voices.

I threw my blankets off. I groaned in pain, now unequivocally aware of the broken fingers in my hand. I ran/fell downstairs in search of my friends. I landed and arrived at the bottom and saw everyone in the kitchen. Garrett, Devin, Haden, and Priest were all eating a meal together. It was a strange sight all around.

Devin and Priest stood at once, and Devin waved him off as he came to get me. I must have looked like a deer in headlights, because he slowed his approach when he reached me. I wasn't entirely aware I was lying on the floor until he was towering several feet above me, instead of the usual few inches.

"What are you doing out of bed? You still look half asleep," he said, pulling me to my feet.

"I thought you all left me," I muttered, looking at Priest over his shoulder. He was still standing, waiting for the instant he was needed. I wanted to go to him, but this time I wanted to hug him, or kiss him, or maybe just slap him. At least I didn't want to hit him anymore.

"We aren't going to leave you, Lenore," Devin said, not quite able to cover the frustrated fatigue in his voice. He helped me back to my room and set me on my bed while he dug through my bedside table drawer.

"You all hate me, don't you?" The quiet question stilled his search.

"Haden explained to us what you figured out. She said you think this wasn't an accident, that it was murder."

"Yes, Adrian Dorn planned it."

He took in a deep breath and let it out like he couldn't rid himself of it fast enough. "I can't help but wonder if this could have all been avoided if you had just stayed away from him from the very beginning."

I wasn't sure how he had come to that conclusion, but I was certain he didn't understand what Dorn was capable of. "Dorn is more dangerous than even you're giving him credit for."

"Then why didn't you stay away from him?" He was scolding me, but he couldn't bring himself to look at me. I debated how to respond to that, but decided the only way for everyone to understand the threat laid down at our door was for everyone to take credit in its creation.

"If you would have left me alone I could have read Adrian's intentions and stopped August from competing altogether." His eyes finally met mine with questions I couldn't answer for myself, let alone him. "I can't be sure if this was an attack specific to August, or if they wanted to draw attention to their purpose. The mayor will use this as an example. He'll want to destroy all the grim down to extinction. He's already collecting them from surrounding counties."

"Good," he said flatly.

I nodded, but I still wasn't sure. Something about that was wrong, I just couldn't see why yet. Maybe the threat of the grim was the only thing keeping the human chaos under wraps. Maybe we needed the distraction to keep us from killing each other. "We'll see."

Devin looked down at my hand. "Does it hurt?"

"Immensely," I said as it re-announced itself with another round of throbbing.

"Garrett had some antibiotics with him, and pain pills, but they're pretty strong. You've been out most of the day. You want another round, or just the OTC?"

"Will you be here when I wake up?" I asked.

He nodded and pulled out the pill bottles. Once I was properly medicated, he tucked me in. I asked him to stay until I was asleep, and as far as I remember, he did.

Two Out of Three Ain't Bad

G ARRETT WAS THE LAST person I wanted to see when I woke up. I hadn't anticipated seeing him more than a few minutes after the tournament, so this should have been a treat, but it wasn't. I already knew he would be the hardest person to convince I had done everything I could to save his sister.

He was sitting in an old rocking chair by my outcropped window section. He had carefully moved the stuffed animals that someone, once upon a time, cared deeply for. It was dark and the only reason I knew it was him was the faint outline of his head against the moonlight streaming in the window.

I tried to sit up, but forgot about the broken fingers and yelped. I sucked air through my teeth and lay back down. When I looked back at him, he hadn't moved. That was about right for him. My pain never did worry him much.

"Did you even realize at the time you broke them?" he asked.

"No, I didn't feel any pain until we got back. I was numb, in more ways than one." I shifted in search of my alarm clock, but it was blinking from a power outage. "What time is it?" I asked.

"About 3 a.m," he mumbled.

It was officially the second morning after August had died. Miraculously the sun was still going to keep rising without her. That shouldn't have been possible. "Have you come to tell me how disappointed you are? Or have Haden and Devin convinced you I was doing everything I could to save her."

"They've explained everything thoroughly. I think they see now, that they are just as much to blame for letting themselves be distracted. I'm not convinced you did everything you could, though."

"Oh really?" I denied myself the luxury of defending myself against his accusation. "And what chess pieces would you have moved differently if you were the master of the universe?"

"For one, I would have installed a shut-off switch to that smart-ass mouth of yours." I tensed at the anger in his voice. If this was going to get physical I was going to need every advantage, especially with a bum hand. "For another, I wouldn't have danced around trying to train you for six months before I called in someone else to do it."

His anger was bleeding over to August. He was blaming me for not saving her and her for not training me well enough to save her. "I suppose you would have chained me in the backyard and refused to feed me until I could shoot straight."

"Don't mock me. You are both to blame for this. Your stubbornness and her damned patience with it."

"What do you think would have happened if she was that hard on me right away?" I paused long enough to let him think, but not answer. "What happened the night you tried to push me too hard, too fast?" I paused again, letting the memory of that night come back to him. "I ran, Garrett. I would have run from her. I never wanted to be the hero. I'm still not sure I want to be, but I've lost my options to do anything else and I've already made my commitments."

"That's just it, isn't it? You've been dragging your feet the whole way. She dragged you into this. I at least got you to walk, but you never did get a good running start. If you had just tried sooner. If you would have accepted your fate and done as we asked."

"Then we would still be here, Garrett. Adrian would still have plotted against her. She would still be dead at the hands of a third grim neither one of us could stop. Nothing could have changed this outcome. Your sister is dead because of Adrian Dorn. And I couldn't save her." He shook his head, still denying me a calmly negotiated win. I decided it was his turn to share the blame.

"I knew I couldn't save her, Garrett. I told all of you that from the very beginning. I'm not the fucking hero! No one listened! I was lazy! I was stubborn! I was everything but *right*!" I paused to rein in my volume so I didn't wake the whole house. "Well, now I have proof that I was right. But you know what pisses me off, more than being right after all of you said I was wrong? You are rationalizing your confidence in me, by belittling my efforts to live up to your expectations."

Garrett rubbed his hands over his face. "I need to hate you right now," he said, looking at me. I couldn't see his eyes but I imagined they were burning with anger, just as they were right after August died.

"That's okay," I answered and lay back on my pillow. I pulled the sheets up and waited to hear him leave, but he didn't and I didn't ask him to.

Back from the Dead

I WOKE AGAIN AT sunup. I woke again at sunup. Garrett was gone and by the looks of the three closed bedroom doors, I assumed he was now sleeping in August's old room. Haden and Devin were late sleepers so I didn't expect them to be up for a while. I was relieved by that. I wasn't ready to face them yet. Not together, at least.

With nearly a full 24 hours' worth of drugged-up sleep, my hand was starting to feel better, but my stomach was yelling at me for not eating. I tiptoed downstairs so I didn't wake anyone. I swung around the stair pillar and jumped the last three steps into the living room.

Priest was sitting on the couch reading. He looked up at my playful entrance and smiled. The room smelled like pine from the toasty fire he had started. While he looked like an advertisement from L.L. Bean, I was painfully aware that I was wearing my Hello Kitty pajamas. Devin apparently had no qualms about dressing me.

I opened my mouth to say something, but I wasn't sure where to start. I was still mad, but I also wanted to curl up against him and cry. In the back of my mind I wanted to do other things with him, but he had already made it clear he wasn't interested in that from me, so I ignored it.

"You look a little more spirited today," he said, setting down his book on the coffee table. "How's the hand?"

I looked at my hand, searching for the answer to his question. "Good," I managed to say.

His smile faded and he stood up. "Lenore." He stepped around the coffee table to meet me. I could see my necklace hanging from his neck with the same bootlace I had put with it. "Devin and Haden explained what happened. I'm so sorry. I didn't mean to let you think I was dead. I just took your advice."

I didn't say anything. I couldn't remember what I had said. I said so many things to him. I assumed he wasn't listening.

"I did need to get out of there, but it was hard to walk away, so I burned it down. I couldn't go back then, even if I wanted to."

"Why did you disappear?"

"I didn't really disappear. I went away to sober up, like I told you I would. I'm clean now. I have been for a while. I came as soon as I heard about August. Lenore, I'm so sorry."

I nodded. "Me too."

He took another step forward. "I'm sorry I left, but I'm here now. For as long as you need me." He looked me over and very slowly put his arm around me and drew me into a hug. It took a moment for his warmth to melt my frigid attitude. When it did, I latched onto him and held on for dear life.

I assumed at some point he would draw me back, but he never did. He held me for over a minute, letting me squeeze the air out of him. I didn't have any tears left to cry at the moment, but part of me wished I did, so I had an excuse to hang on a little longer.

Who's in Charge

THE NEXT FEW DAYS were a series of awkward conversations and business as usual. None of us seemed to know where to begin without August. I knew I was supposed to be the leader now, but how do you go from being the deadweight lackey to the boss overnight? What's more, who could respect you for it, when someone had to die to make it happen?

"I think we should start your training again," Garrett said abruptly at lunch one day.

I stopped my grilled cheese inches from my wide mouth. "What?" I stared at the closed-mouthed man across from me. Apart from the occasional question about my hand or an *"excuse me"* as he made his way around me in the kitchen, Garrett had not spoken to me since he told me he hated me.

"August wanted you in the tournament finale. Your archery will get you into it, but you can't rely on that to get you a win in the final competition. You'll need to work on your hand to hand, your aim with a gun, and I think I'll get you trained with a few other weapons, just in case."

I looked to Haden catty-corner to me. She looked to Devin beside me, and he looked back to me. Apparently, I wasn't the only one blindsided by this. Priest was at the far end of the table against the wall, sitting on a newly added folding chair. He kept to himself in these conversations, since he knew he didn't have any say in the outcome.

I cleared my throat and put down my sandwich. "I believe I've missed a step, Garrett. You do realize Adrian Dorn, the one that designs and runs the tournament, just killed one of us during a tournament. Why exactly would we ever go back there?"

"Don't you want him dead? Don't you want revenge on my sister's killer?"

I looked around the table again. I was treading on thin ice, and I was already carrying a bowling ball's worth of guilt. "I want answers, Garrett, and I can't get them if he's dead, or if I'm dead."

"Fuck answers!" *Crack* goes the ice. "If you knew he killed her, you should have struck him down that night!" *Splash*.

"I don't fully understand Dorn, so I'm not going to announce that I'm his enemy until I have to."

"How do you plan to understand him? Flirt your way into his bed? I bet you'll understand him pretty well then!"

I glanced at Devin, and he raised his hands, refusing to take fault for that particular interpretation. "I'll figure something out. Right now, I'm running on instincts."

"Fat lot of good they've done you so far," Garrett mumbled.

I chose to ignore the attack. He still needed time to figure out I wasn't to blame, and neither was he. "I know what August was concerned about. I know she thought the grim can take our souls."

"Souls?" Priest finally looked up.

I nodded. "It's complicated, but August thought the demons taking over the grim will eventually get strong enough to override humans and take their souls." This appeared to be news for Priest, but not for Haden and Devin. I wondered how much they knew, but had been sworn to secrecy by August.

"All the more reason to get into the tournament and kill a bunch of grim," Garrett said.

"I'm not sure if I agree with that," I said.

"What?" Garrett asked it, but three more brows furrowed in my direction.

"I just need more information. I'm missing a piece of this puzzle."

"What puzzle?" Garrett hissed.

"Is no one questioning why Adrian Dorn killed August?" I asked. "Why doesn't he want the best swordsman in his finale to kill a bunch of grim? Isn't the mayor's whole purpose with this tournament to kill grim? Was this just a political power play for advertisement? If so, for what purpose? Let's face it, the ladder to the top is meaningless now. With only about a third of the population left, they aren't looking for revenue. I know you are all hot to get vengeance, but I'm not interested in killing Adrian Dorn until I know why he killed August."

Everyone stared blankly at me for a moment. Priest finally spoke. "So, what is your plan?"

I glanced at everyone, seeking permission to offer it. No one seemed displeased with my gall to offer one, so I proceeded. "As I said, I need to keep Adrian off my scent. I don't think he views me as a threat since he didn't distract me that night, but that might have changed. I'll assume it hasn't since I didn't succeed. I would like to go to another tournament. One none of us is competing in. I need to touch him for more than a few seconds." Garrett narrowed his eyes. I rolled my eyes in response. "It doesn't need to involve bodily fluids."

"How will touching him help you figure him out?" Priest asked. Everyone seemed to have the same question.

"I don't really understand it, but I feel something when I touch him. It's very... unnerving." Everyone still stared at me blankly. I couldn't tell if they believed me or not. "At one of the barn dances a while back I touched an old man. I instantly felt the sickening pleasure he got from raping women in his youth."

"So, you're psychic now?" Haden asked, looking a little concerned.

I smiled thinly. "No, I don't think it's like that. I think I can sniff out the bad guys. I think I can sense people's evil intentions."

"In that case, we'll start training before your hand heals." Garrett stood up and took his dishes to the sink.

"Garrett, I'm not—"

"Look!" He swung back a shaking finger to me. "I've already lost my sister to this asshole! I'm not losing anyone else I care about!" My objection fled my mind as I realized he was only trying to protect me.

"I second that," Devin said, putting an arm around me. "Garrett's right, Lenore." I regarded him with disappointed shock that he, of all people, would agree with Garrett. "I don't want you anywhere near this guy unless you are fully prepared mentally and physically." Devin stood and stared down Garrett. "However, this time, I'll be helping with the training to make sure we don't add to your scars."

Garrett strode back to the table to confront him. I got to my feet in case I needed to fan out the fires of testosterone. Tensed and ready for an attack, Garrett took a moment to admire his paranoid creation before turning his attention to Devin. "You haven't had a chance to see her in action close up, have you?"

I wasn't sure if Garrett intended to add innuendo in the statement, but Devin certainly seemed to take it that way. His chest puffed up and his biceps flexed as he resisted the urge to vault past me and wring Garrett's beefy neck.

"I look forward to seeing if you can handle her. Even I couldn't keep up with her energy in the end. I have a few scars myself, in fact." He glanced at me and winked. Rather than participate in this battle of the cocks, I walked away leaving them to figure out who should be beating the crap out of me, or sleeping with me—whichever that discussion was supposedly about.

Barn Dance II

AFTER SOME VERY HEATED glares across the living room between Devin and Garrett, Haden caught my eye and smiled at me. I smiled back instinctively, but furrowed my brow at the unusual pleasantry. "You know what we need, Lenore?" She gleamed impishly.

"What's that, Haden?" I said, putting down my magazine. It was over three years old, but I still liked to pretend people gave a shit about which accessories went with what outfits.

"We need new men, old beer, less clothing, and more sex."

"I imagine we do." I grinned playfully at Haden. I was happy she was at least talking to me, let alone joking with me. "But where will we get such things."

"Jimmy said there's a barn dance not far from here. Come on." She jumped out of her chair and pulled me off the couch. She was always stronger than I anticipated. "I'll help you get out of these clothes," she taunted the three stunned men with a smack on my rear that, as usual, was a little too hard.

After we had changed into less clothing and put on a ridiculous amount of makeup and perfume, we came back down to find three well-dressed men with coats on, waiting to escort us to the dance. Haden laughed and crossed her arms. "What the hell is this?"

"You two are not going to a barn dance looking like that without me." Devin crossed his arms right back at Haden. I could see his chivalry had now fully translated into paternalistic protection and was even bordering on controlling.

Priest cleared his throat and stepped in front of Devin to interject. "I believe what Devin is trying to say is, that you ladies look so lovely you will undoubtedly attract men of a predatory nature. If you would like, we could escort you to your evening festivities and safeguard you both from any unsavory advances." Priest went so far as to kiss each of our hands, which made my heart flutter. It was unusual to see anyone out flirt Devin.

"Well, at last, a *real* gentleman." Haden glared at Devin, who no doubt took the insult like a kick to the balls. Priest opened the door for us, and Haden headed out. I gave him a raised index finger asking for a minute, and he headed out.

Garrett followed them and paused at the door. "You look nice." Again with the *nice*.

"Thank you," I said before heading over to Devin. "You know she's just trying to make you jealous, right?"

"Yeah, but I hate that she can do it so easily." I smiled and hugged him. "What was that for?"

"For taking care of me. For forgiving me. For defending me. And for just being you."

"Was Garrett serious this morning about having scars from you?"

"I don't know about scars, but I did do a good number on his face one night." Devin smiled at me and leaned in for a kiss. I pulled back and put up a finger.

"Be nice, it took me three tries to get the lip liner just right." He smirked at me mischievously, but I raised my brow in warning, and he settled for a peck. He then hooked my elbow in his and escorted me to Priest's SUV, which could easily fit all five of us.

Till we meet again

THE BARN DANCE WAS in a hall instead of a barn, but the beer was cold, the food was prepackaged, and the music was loud, so no one cared. Despite Haden's grand display, she made no attempts to keep up her flirtation with Priest. In the end, he sat off to one side like a wallflower drinking a juice box. From my spot on the dance floor with Devin, I could see him fiddling with the necklace charm I had made him.

"What are you smiling at?" Devin looked down at me.

"I'm smiling at the pleasure of dancing with you, of course," I said, showing him a toothy smile that he mirrored.

"Yeah, right." He glanced back at Priest. "You seem pretty happy to have him back."

I shrugged. "I guess. I didn't realize I missed him so much, until he was back."

"I know the feeling. The heart tends to play catch-up." I nodded in agreement. "What about Garrett? Are you happy he's here?" he asked begrudgingly. He obviously still didn't approve of our relationship. Whatever it might be.

I paused, thinking about that. "I think so." Devin frowned at the struggle in my conviction. "It was different when we were alone. Or maybe it wasn't. I don't even know if he likes me. I know he's not interested in anything serious. In fact, I'm surprised he hasn't run back to Chicago already."

"I'm sure he will eventually. The question is, can you be okay with that?"

I shrugged again. "I don't like the way relationships work in the new world."

"I know," he murmured and rubbed my back. "I wish I could make it easier for you, but you won't let me."

I furrowed my brow. "Devin, if I slept with you now, I'd be hopelessly in love with you and I'd never be able to function outside of your arms."

He smiled, but part of him looked sad. He leaned in close to me. "Remind me what the downside of that is?"

"No downside, but Haden is already hopelessly in love with you, and you don't need any more women vying for your attentions."

He laughed heartily. "Again, why not?"

I shook my head. "You really have no shame, do you?"

"No, not where beautiful women are concerned." He pulled me in close. "And you are definitely that." He dipped me and I squealed and laughed. For his enjoyment alone, he kept me down there helpless to get back up.

I could see the room upside down, but when the legs parted, I saw a familiar face. A face that made my skin crawl. Noting my displeasure, Devin pulled my upright. "What's wrong?" He looked around for the source of my spoiled in demeanor.

"Thank you for the dance." I kissed his cheek and abandoned him in puzzlement.

I found Haden dancing with a short man in glasses. He didn't look to be her type, but he was handsome and fit enough to be useful in bed. I tapped her on the shoulder and Haden glared at me for the interruption. Reading the gravity of my mood she dropped her attitude and pulled away from her dance partner to give me her full attention. "What's up?"

"I need your gun." I tried to sound composed, but I was asking for a gun.

She perked her brow and glanced around the room, but she didn't hesitate to hand it to me from her ankle holster. "Need any help?"

"Nah, I got it." I nodded to the short man in apology for the interruption. He nodded and pulled Haden back to him. He was apparently not a talker. That was nice... for Haden.

I could see Garrett eyeing me from over his dance partner. She was a short, skinny blonde. If I had a mind to, I could kick her ass, but there wasn't much point in winning a prize that didn't want to be won. The only reason he was paying attention now, was because he thought there was danger afoot.

I shook my head at him to let him know there was no problem. I crossed over to the food table in search of my target. The old man had been happily grazing the snack table. He especially liked to watch the cleavage-baring women lean across the table for a preferred chip or cracker. Everything about the former rapist incited me.

He spotted me coming toward the table and let his eyes trace me from the legs up. When he reached my face it took a moment for him to remember me, but he did. The memory clicked, as did his recognition of the expression on my face and the gun in my hand.

He scrambled toward the side door, spilling more than a few people's beers on the way.

He didn't move fast and nearly fell twice trying to keep up the pace. Had he been capable of running, he might have died of a heart attack. I almost felt sorry for him, but then I remembered the fear and trauma he had induced in his victims. I had no reason to sympathize for a rapist simply because he was too feeble to harm anyone anymore.

I crossed by the punchbowl, getting a few wary glances. When they caught sight of the gun at my side, sustenance ceased to be important and they shuffled out of my way. The side door popped open and the old man made his escape. Despite his frantic efforts, I made it to the door right after him.

I propped it open and stepped out into the darkness. I watched him limp toward the tree line for safety. I didn't bother giving chase. There was no point. I didn't need to explain myself or lord my disgust over him. He knew what he was. I knew what he was. And we both knew what I would do to him the next time I saw him.

I aimed.

I fired.

He fell.

Mentally Washing my Hands

I WAS SURPRISED MY weapons fire only managed to still the dance floor for a little while. I returned Haden's gun to her and she burned with the same questions everyone else did. Instead of asking them, she took a different path. "How'd she do for you?" she asked, placing the weapon back in her ankle holster.

"Fine weapon you have there," I said.

She nodded and I went on my way. Devin had found a new dance partner, so I joined Priest on the folding chairs. I caught Devin's eye on the way by and he mouthed, "*You okay?*" I nodded back with a small smile.

Priest looked relaxed despite the hard chairs. I sat down next to him, pulling the chair out a little so I wasn't right on top of him. He regarded me coolly. He was likely still figuring out how to react to me shooting random men at dances.

"Was that the old rapist you had referenced earlier?" he finally asked.

"Yup," I said.

"He seemed to know you intended to kill him."

"Yup, that was the bargain I struck when I let him live the first time." I could see him trying to figure out whether he was okay with that or not. "He hurt a lot of people, Priest. Young, vibrant women lost a lot more than their innocence to him. They lost trust, hope, and even their faith, because of his desire to stick his dick somewhere he didn't have permission to."

I could feel him watching me. "Okay," he said approvingly. I looked at him and he nodded at me, bestowing a metaphorical pat on my back for my justice, belated as it was. I hadn't questioned my right to kill the bastard, but I was glad to have Priest's approval.

"Priest—" I started, but he leaned forward and interrupted me.

"Lenore, my name is Matthew," he said sternly. "When are you going to start calling me that?"

I shook my head. "I can't call you that."

"Why not?" he asked, raising his brow. "I'm not a priest anymore, remember? I'm just a man now. I would like to hear my name from your lips."

My heart was thumping hard, at this suggestion, but I shook my head. I couldn't very well explain to him how intimate his name seemed to me now. I would have sooner called him 'sir' than Matthew. "I just can't yet."

His eyes danced over me like he was trying to read me, but couldn't quite make out the words. I leaned back in my chair and crossed my arms. I remembered that the action accentuated my cleavage in my low-cut top, so I put my arms down. Not that Priest would have noticed, either way.

Confessional

"P UNCH?" PRIEST RETURNED WITH my pink punch and put it in my face. I snapped out of my Garrett-spying and took the pink concoction. Priest sat down with his own glass and waited for me to drink.

"What?" I raised an eyebrow at his observance.

"I'm waiting for you to tell me if there's any alcohol in it."

"Oh." I suddenly felt bad for him. I wasn't a big drinker, so I was familiar with what it was like being the only sober one at a party. "Sorry."

"Don't be sorry. I've had enough fun for two lifetimes." I stared at him wondering if any of what he had done prior to now was fun. He motioned for me to drink and I did so. I grimaced. It was not only spiked, but it was distastefully strong.

"It's spiked."

"You can have both then," he said, smiling.

"Actually, it's really bad. I'll find us some sodas." I reached to pinch his cup with my own and take them away.

"It's fine, Lenore." He pulled back his cup.

My fingers slipped, and the release sent my cup splashing back at me and his splashing onto him. My face melted. He was now covered in the noxious substance he was trying to avoid in the first place. His hands levitated uselessly over his cream—now pink—sweater. My blouse though dark enough to hide the stain, was drenched. "I'm sorry."

"I know you are." He looked frustrated even though he was trying to be polite. I closed my eyes and tried not to let my mortification override me. When I opened them his frustration was replaced by a smile. I wasn't sure what had changed, but he wasn't being polite anymore, he was amused. "Come on." He stood up. "I have clothes in my vehicle." He took my hand and led me outside. I wondered what Garrett thought of that, or if he was even watching.

Changing Outfits and Opinions

I**T WAS A GOOD** deal colder outside with a wet top. I was shivering before we got to the Tahoe. Priest popped his hatch and pulled a bin of clothing over to us. He pulled out another sweater, gray this time. He probably wasn't going to risk ruining anything else.

"Lady's choice." He scooted the bin toward me while he stripped off his sweater. I couldn't help but appreciate the view of his trim and now healthy frame. He was in desperate need of a tan, but I didn't have room to talk. Our hard winters were known to harvest pale skin.

I dug through the bin and found a blue sweater similar in color to my current top. I hoped that would make my change of attire less obvious. I pulled my blouse off over my head, not bothering to turn around or ask Priest to do so. I was well aware the cold air was leaving little to the imagination behind my bra.

He caught my eye as I arranged the sweater to pull over my head. He was scolding me with his set jaw, but I could tell he was appreciating some of what he was seeing since he wasn't turning away. I ignored his judgment and raised my arms well over my head to slip the sweater on. I pulled it on slowly, offering him as much of a view as he could stand before I popped my head through and tugged it down over my hips.

I opened my mouth to ask how I looked, but I could see his expression had changed from scolding appreciation to astonished fury. I already knew what he had seen to change his mood. I mentally kicked myself for being so stupid. "Priest..." I didn't have anything to say after that, but he wasn't listening.

He moved to me and lifted the sweater to look at my belly. I had received eight small puncture wounds thanks to a grill fork that kept evading my defenses. None of them were close to being lethal, but they did leave nasty scars. "These are the scars Devin was referring to?" I nodded.

He circled around to my back and lifted the sweater over my shoulders to observe the scars from sword fights where I neglected to keep my enemy engaged. I had no idea how many were there, but after one such fight, Garrett had insisted I sleep on my stomach for several nights, and even watched me the first night, to make sure I did so.

"Jesus Christ!" He hissed the blasphemy more than yelled it. He released my sweater and came back to face me. He looked at my head scar which most people missed without a close-up view. "Is that all?"

"My legs," I answered and he looked over my jeans like he might be able to see through the fabric. I started to undo them so we could finish the examination, but he stopped my hands, holding them at my waist.

"How many?"

"Just a few. One big one from a bullet graze." His eyes widened and I thought he might explode if he had to hear one more thing. "Garrett wanted me to see how hard it would be to fight with even a flesh wound from a gun." It was my attempt to explain Garrett's reasoning, but it went over like gasoline to fire. Intentionally shooting me would have seemed extreme to me early in my training, but after so many lessons in the form of injuries, a close shave with a bullet seemed on par with the progression.

Priest shook his head in disbelief. He was shaking with anger and I thought I might need to tackle him so he didn't try to go after Garrett, but instead he pulled me into his arms and kissed my cheek and temple.

"I knew there would be cuts and bruises. I knew you had to get hurt, but..." He drew me back suddenly to look at me. "I never would have let you go back with that son of a bitch if I knew it would be like this. Even a lecherous drunken priest would have been safer than that."

I didn't know what to say to him. He was about six months late to offer me sympathy for my scars. I had come to terms with the method of their infliction, and the purpose. I just kept forgetting that everyone else hadn't gotten there yet.

"How can you even stand being near him? I've never killed a man, but I'm considering it now."

I gripped his arms and shook my head. "I don't want him dead."

Priest winced and drew away from me. "No," he said, denying his own conclusion. "You don't care for him, do you?"

I didn't know what to say to that either. I had been with Garrett for three months, day and night. He had spent as much time healing my wounds and cooking me meals as he had beating the hell out of me. Even if our sexual relationship could be summed up as a one-night stand and a drug-induced bathroom tryst, I couldn't discount my desire to expand our relationship.

"Lenore, did you and he... Tell me you didn't sleep with him." I couldn't believe how awful he was making me feel. I felt like I should be wearing a scarlet letter: "W" for whore. I was probably the only person I knew who had gotten laid twice since the apocalypse, with the same person, and was going to be shamed for it.

I stepped away from him, trying to hide my embarrassment. "Thanks for the sweater. I'll try not to spill anything else on it." I moved around the driver's side to head into the building. Priest shut the back and met me via the passenger's side.

"He tried to rape you," he summed up his objection to a relationship between Garrett and me.

"He was pretending to rape me, we established that. I wouldn't have... Fuck, Priest, leave this alone! It's not like I was sleeping with him the whole time. I wasn't getting off on him beating me or anything." He visibly relaxed as if he was starting to see some silver lining to his horrific interpretation.

"There was a lot of between stuff. I was alone with him, and I didn't know when I would see my friends again. He wasn't... I have needs too, you know," I blurted out in a panicked defense. "Twice!" I held up my fingers to bring home the point. "Only twice, with him, that's it."

He seemed to regard that as something to add to his relief.

"How many women have you had? You aren't exactly in the hierarchy of virtue either!" I crossed my arms, comfortable that my cleavage was now fully covered. His face fell and he offered me sympathy, or pity—it was hard to tell which at that point.

"Lenore, I'm not criticizing your desire to be with a man. You're a grown woman, and a beautiful one. You should have a lover—many if you like. But I'm having trouble consolidating the image of a man who could inflict those wounds, and one that could earn the right to lie in your bed."

I took in a deep breath and tried to figure that out myself. I felt the answer, but I didn't know how to formulate it into words. When I saw Priest patiently awaiting my answer, I knew how to explain it.

I licked my lips and came closer to him so I didn't have to speak any louder than necessary. "Do you remember the last time I saw you, before you burned down the church?" He didn't nod, but his eyes shifted down so I knew he did. "You held me." He nodded. "I... I wept so hard. I thought I was never going to stop. You let me feel it without judgement and when I was done, I felt free... of everything. It was humiliating and emotionally excruciating and humbling, but it was cathartic. When I was finally settled and calm... I kissed you."

He took in a deep breath. Just the mention of it made him as uncomfortable as me, although probably for different reasons. I hugged myself tighter, trying to protect myself his indifference.

"I was in so much pain, and then I wasn't, and you were there. I was grateful you let me feel all of that and didn't shove me away or try to rush me through it. At that moment, I wanted to..." I laughed, thinking that the obvious ending to that sentence would have ruined the tone of my speech. "I wanted to absorb you." I frowned, hoping he could understand that. "Not just you, your body, but every part of you. I wanted so much to return your generosity somehow. I didn't know any other way to do that, so I threw myself at you."

He nodded, taking in that information. I still hadn't answered his question, so I continued.

"With Garrett, I had gone through three months of intense physical and emotional changes. I hated him so much, but in the end it was only him and me. He may have inflicted all these scars, but he was also the one who stitched me up. He carried me to my bed when I was too sore to walk up the steps. He never once insinuated himself into my bed. The only time we were together, was when *I* wanted to be with him."

I couldn't tell what Priest thought of this. He seemed to be more relaxed than he was before. He may not have approved, but at least I had convinced him I wasn't off my rocker.

"I don't know how to explain my feelings for Garrett, because I'm not really sure myself. But I do know this: I wish he was dancing with me in there instead of with that blonde."

"Okay," was all he said in response to my heartfelt confession.

Crazy

P RIEST DISAPPEARED INTO THE crowd after we came back in. Devin swung his partner to the outskirts, where I was standing, so he could talk to me. "What was that all about?" he said, eyeing my new sweater.

"I spilled spiked pink punch on a recovering alcoholic." I gave him a thumbs-up. "Yeah, I'm that suave." Devin laughed at my antics and twirled his partner back into the crowd.

I stared over to the vacant folding chairs, debating whether I wanted to join the rank of wallflower. I quickly calculated what my chances of getting home alive were if I went out into the small town in search of a functional abandoned car. We usually took multiple vehicles to parties so I could drive home early after I surrendered to the flight part of my fight-or-flight instincts, but this time we all piled into Priest's well-heated mammoth. I had no escape plan—how unlike me.

As I rubbed my neck to ease the stress headache forming at the base of my skull, a bottle of soda popped into my line of sight. I turned and saw Priest holding it out to me. "I thought a bottle was best. Neck hurt?" he asked, noting my position.

I took the bottle. "Thank you. I thought you'd left me to seek out more conciliatory conversation." I popped the top to the soda and took a sip.

"Nope, I prefer my conversations like my women: provocative."

I could feel myself blush, and I looked away to hide it. When I looked back, he was still watching me, amused. A moment of silence passed before he nodded to the chairs. "Would you sit with me?"

Even if I had any preference to standing, I would have sat anyway because of how he asked it. I hadn't known Priest as a priest, but I imagined his manners and compassion suited his profession well. It made me sad to wonder why God had left him here, but I was selfishly happy He did.

"What's happening in that mind of yours?" he asked when he caught me watching him.

"I was just wondering how life was treating you. You weren't very happy with me prior to your sobriety."

"No, I wasn't." He took a deep breath and let it out slowly. "I was angry at God, and then I was angry at myself. It was a vicious cycle of self-neglect, purposeful sinning, and shameful prostration. And then you came along and…"

He paused like he was remembering something about our first meeting. To my knowledge it wasn't meaningful in any way. He was rude, curt, and practically spat at me for suggesting he bless my water for me. In the end, he did it, but was neither happy nor accommodating about it.

"I remember the look you gave me when you weren't afraid of me anymore. I also remember your explanation for it. You called me apocalyptic road kill." He laughed and I smiled even though it wasn't a happy memory. "You said I disgusted you because despite what I had become, I still thought I was better than you."

I looked away, trying not to induce any more bad memories. He turned my chin back to look at him. "You were right." His eyes locked onto mine and it felt comfortable. "I did think that. I thought because I served God, I should have had a better seat than everyone else. I realize now I might still have a purpose to serve while I'm still on this Earth, but it won't be to lord over anyone. It will be to stand beside them.

"I know you'll have to discuss it with Haden and Devin, but I would like to stand with you. I'd like to help in whatever minor way I can. Holy water, clean sweaters, whatever; you name it, I'll do it. If you'll have me."

I was floored by the offer. I was thrilled he was back, but I never assumed he would stay, permanently. I chuckled. "Wow, I feel like I should be putting my hand out for a ring or something." He smiled. "Um, of course, I'll discuss it with Haden and Devin. I don't think they'll mind. We might want to consider looking for a bigger house if Garrett's going to be hanging around too." I glanced out at the crowd.

"Is there any particular reason why?" I asked. "I mean, I'm sure your intentions are noble, but how does one go from, *'leave me alone so I can sober up,'* to *'hey can I join your team.'*"

He looked down and took my hands in his. He swallowed hard. I took in a deep breath to prepare for the serious nature of what he was about to say. "Do you remember—I know you do, but I just wanted to stick with the format of tonight's conversations." I laughed, letting it take the edge off my nervousness. He squeezed my hands and cleared his throat before starting again. "That day I slapped you."

I nodded, pinching back my lips so I didn't accidentally smile out of discomfort.

"You thought I did it because you cursed the lord's name. I told you it was because you called me nuts." He shifted uncomfortably. "I was back from the brink of death. I was going through withdrawals."

"I know." I squeezed his hands and he shook his head.

"It's no excuse, and now knowing *all* that you had been through, I can't even imagine how disappointed in me you were."

"Priest, stop. After everything I had been through, that slap was nothing to me. I knew you hated yourself for it the second you did it. You aren't Garrett. Don't ever think I would assume you're capable of that." He nodded and offered a glare out to the dance floor. I couldn't see Garrett, but I assumed he was in amongst the expanding mass of dancers.

"Anyway, I never explained to you why it bothered me so much. Truthfully, I probably never would have until I heard you talking about your ability to read the evil in people."

I raised my brow. "Oh, don't tell me, you're my polar opposite and you can read the good in people."

He tipped his head and frowned. "Kind of like that."

"Kind of? Can we get matching superhero suits or what?"

He licked his lips and I could feel his palms sweating, but I didn't let go of his hands. "Lenore, for a long time I thought I *was* crazy. Before the apocalypse..." He took in a deep breath and I could hear how shaky it was.

"Priest, you can tell me anything. I'm your friend. I won't judge you. I won't accuse you of being crazy. I've already experienced enough weirdness to know I'm not the foremost authority on sanity."

"Thank you." He seemed to relax and go into information mode rather than emotional overload. "Before the apocalypse I started hearing God." He paused, letting his first statement sink in. It didn't sink so much as linger in my brain until more information was acquired to direct it to the proper file.

"I don't mean hear Him like hearing the call of God, or God spoke to me through my dream, or I saw a sign and knew God meant for me to do this. I mean the clouds part and God speaks. The bush burns and His voice is in me and around me." He stopped like it was the end of the story, but I knew he was just waiting for me to catch up and show some sign of support.

"What did He say to you?" I could tell from his expression that it wasn't an appropriate question. Apparently, what is spoken between a man and his God is private. "Sorry."

"No, it's fine, but it's hard to explain, because it's an emotional and conceptual communication. To say God spoke to me is deceiving. It's like if I wanted to dance with you I could ask you, or I could stand up and offer my hand. You would understand to take my hand and follow." I looked to the dance floor, wondering if dancing sounded like more fun than talking about nonverbal conversations with deities.

"Did he tell you the world was going to end?"

"No." Priest rubbed his forehead. "I can't explain it, but He made me feel important. He made me feel loved and safe. I was happy beyond all explanation, and then He was gone. The apocalypse came and He was gone. Completely. No parting of the clouds. No dreams. Nothing. I was alone and not just one-fucking-set-of-footprints alone."

I could hear the bitterness I was all too familiar with coming back into his voice. His hands started to pull away from mine, but I grabbed on tighter. He may not have wanted to hold my hands while he felt this pain again, but I wanted to hold his.

"He was so vacant from my life I couldn't even remember why I became a priest. I knew what my vows were. I understood the job, but I couldn't even remember what it felt like to want God in my life. I know you understand loss, but now imagine if you couldn't remember how you felt being near August." I frowned at the mention of her name, but I tried to stay with the conversation so I could understand him. "Imagine if you had every physical memory of her, but without the emotional memory of loving her. You remembered laughing at her jokes, but you have no idea why they were funny. You remembered hugging her, but you have no idea what compelled you to do so."

I could feel Priest squeezed my hands, willing me to understand. I nodded and looked down to remind him that I was, in fact, a live being and not a stress ball. He glanced down and released my hands. I stretched them out and tried to touch him again in some way to show my support, but he turned and spoke out to the crowd as if I wasn't there.

"Knowing that I did feel something but not being able to remember it was worse than being abandoned. I could have forgiven Him for leaving me behind, but erasing my memory of my love for Him? That was beyond cruel. That was a violation. I couldn't and wouldn't understand it. I tried to hear Him. I prayed. I begged. I performed ritualistic offerings that bordered on witchcraft.

"Eventually, I gave up. I started out doing everything I had missed out on in life. I ate to excess, I fucked to excess, and I did drugs to excess." He paused and I could see him contemplating something else. I waited patiently. He had offered me time to explain myself. I would do the same for him.

"Getting back to your question about why I want to join you." His eyes flickered over mine and he wet his lips. "Being near you, especially sober, I can feel what it was that compelled me to love God. I always bless you, because around you I feel inspired to do so. You're like this little light in the dark. I can't see all the light and I can't ever feel the way I did when He was speaking to me, but I do thank Him for you."

I stood up. I wasn't aware until that moment I wanted to. Or rather desperately needed to. "I'm going to step outside for some air. I'll be right back," I said before escaping the conversation.

Fear

SHIT. *HOLY SHIT.*

I took a few sobering inhalations of cold air, wishing that I smoked. The fowl stench of toxic smoke burning my lungs was just what I needed. Something to take the edge off a man telling me I was, literally, his connection to God.

I couldn't help but feel sympathy and, as vividly as he described it, perhaps empathy for his situation. I was more than happy to be his friend, his shoulder to cry on, and his good listener, but I wasn't sure I was prepared to be his peephole to the Creator of heaven and earth. The thought of it made me a little sick to my stomach.

Expectations for my life over the last two years had gone from grocery clerk, 3rd sidekick, useful sidekick, potential hero, secret leader, and now a former priest's consolation prize to God. I really needed to find new friends.

"Wow." Priest stepped outside with me and watched me fluster and fidget.

"Oh, sorry, I just needed to get some air."

"I can see that," he said, moving toward me.

"I'm sorry." I turned to face him, unconsciously backing away from him as quickly as he advanced. "I didn't mean to appear unsympathetic. I completely support you joining the team, and I appreciate you telling me about your conversations. I totally get it, and I believe you. I—"

"Lenore." He stopped moving and so did I. "I've seen you stand between two men about to pummel each other and not flinch except to tense. Why are you backing away from me now?"

I looked around at how much ground I had covered. I wanted to make an excuse, because it was politically correct to do so when you felt uncomfortable about answering honestly. I didn't want to make excuses with Priest, though.

"You're right, I don't scare easily anymore, but what you just said in there... how you were looking at me... That scared the shit out of me." I could hear the tremble in my voice.

"Okay." He nodded and took one apprehensive step forward. "I can see that was too much."

"I'm sorry, I want to support you. I am your friend."

"I know you are." He took another step and I had to resist the urge to back away.

"But I can't be your light, Priest. I can't. That's too much. August asked me to be her hero and I failed at that. I can't be your reason or purpose or hope. I just can't."

"Okay." He took another step and I whimpered, barely able to resist my desire to run away. "We'll just be friends then." He stayed still and let me get used to his proximity, treating me like a wild animal ready to flee. "I'm not asking you to do anything. Do you understand? I have no expectations beyond friendship."

"I'm sorry."

"I'm not mad. I'm not disappointed. I'm just concerned for my friend." He smiled. "When you tell Haden and Devin I want to join the team, you tell them it's because I'm living out of the back of my SUV and I want a place to stay with decent security."

I laughed and nodded. "I think that sounds pathetic enough to play on their sympathies."

"Good." He smiled. I couldn't believe how careful and gentle he was being with me. I was having a mental breakdown weenie-style and he was somehow at ease with it all. He must have been a very good priest.

"I do want you to stay," I added in case that point hadn't been made between him asking and me fleeing the scene.

He nodded, keeping a tame smile on his face. "Lenore?" His head tipped to one side. "May I hold you now?" Once again it wasn't an offer, but a question. I might have wanted to run, but the way he posed the question made it impossible to refuse. He wasn't demanding any-thing from me. He was seeking permission to provide me comfort.

I nodded and moved forward to him. He wrapped his arms around me and I melted against him. I knew it was probably just the memory of our first cathartic embrace, but the instant I was in his arms I felt at ease. He was more than a warm blanket on a cold day; he was a foot rub and a bubble bath all rolled into strong arms and sandalwood soap.

Mental Break

I TOOK ANOTHER TURN on the dance floor with Devin after coming back inside, mostly because I felt I needed some
time away from Priest. So much had already happened tonight—
justifiable murder, intimate revelations—and it was barely after
midnight. Haden wouldn't want to leave before two, and by the
looks of things, we were going to have a few tag-alongs. Assuming
they made it past my evil radar.

"What's going on, Lenore? You seemed to be having a pretty
intense talk with Matthew."

"Yeah." I rolled my eyes to play it down. "You know how
preachy he can get."

"No, not really." Devin shook his head. "Are you alright?"

"I was having a nervous breakdown, but I'm better now." I
smiled warmly and nuzzled into his shoulder.

"I know when you're trying to underplay things, Lenore," he
whispered in my ear.

I looked up at him and sighed. "Can we just not talk for a while?
I've been doing way too much talking tonight."

"If that's what you need." He nodded and ushered my head back to his shoulder. We didn't speak. We just slow-danced to two more songs that should have been danced fast.

Beer Break

HADEN CAUGHT UP WITH me by the snack table and smacked my butt hard. "Ouch!" I rubbed my butt and gawked at her in shock. "Is this going to be a thing for us? Because I seriously think I need a safe word."

"Why aren't you drinking?" she slurred in my face, clearly way drunker than me. "You are supposed to be getting fucked and fucked up, not necessarily in that order."

"Sounds about right from my experience," I grumbled and grabbed a cracker. Haden knocked it out of my hand. "Seriously, you are a violent drunk and you're not exactly butterfly-kisses sober."

"You have to drink with me!" She shoved her finger in my face. "Devin will watch out for us, but you have to drink with me." I was about to explain that Priest couldn't drink so therefore I felt obligated not to drink to keep him company, but her face crumpled, and she looked like she might cry. "It's just you and me now. We're all that's left. We have to stick together. Girl power, you know? They don't get it." She waved out to the three men we arrived with. "We get it. Don't we?"

I wasn't sure I did, but that wasn't the point. "Yeah, we do."

Haden handed me a beer. It was from someone else's hand and they grabbed it right back from her. I waved an apology and took two fresh beers from the cooler on the table. I popped the tab on one and handed it to Haden. She didn't need another beer, but she did need to have one with me. I popped my tab and clunked my can to hers.

"To sisterhood, a bond built by quarrels, but never toppled by them."

Haden nodded at me. I tipped my beer for a quick drink and she did the same. While she was paused in drunken thought I chugged most of my beer down. I took her beer. "Let me get you another one." She nodded vaguely at my offer and didn't notice when I handed her my nearly empty can. "I'm going to go find your man, hang on."

I chugged her remaining beer on the way into the crowd out of respect for the product. I weaved through the dancers with the expert precision of someone who has often had to soberly find my friends and announce my departure. I found Devin, happily entwined with his partner, and tapped on his shoulder.

He turned and smiled at me. "Ready for another dance?" I loved that he didn't pay any heed to his partner's annoyance. His friends would always be his first priority no matter how slutty the newcomer was.

"I'm sorry to spoil your evening, but she's really too drunk to be going home with somebody new." Contrary to my concern for his ruined night, his eyes frantically searched for Haden. "She's by the punch bowl."

"Okay." He nodded and squeezed my shoulder. "I'll take care of it."

"Thank you." I left Devin to explain things to his partner in a way that only he could. By the end of his explanation, she would feel like she was the one being generous enough to release him to help his friend. By the time she even comprehended she had been dumped, Haden's former infatuation would have been sent over to pick up where he left off. The short man with glasses would be more than happy to oblige. Especially after Devin explained Haden's propensity for projectile vomiting. It was that kind of devoted chivalry that made me jealous of Haden.

You Can't Handle the Truth

I PLOPPED DOWN BESIDE Priest without a thought to my tipsy arrival, or how he might feel about it. "And what have you been up to?" he asked.

"Dancing and drinking," I answered proudly.

"I can see that, and smell that." He grimaced.

"Oh, shit!" I covered my mouth. "I'm sorry," I mumbled. "I'll go find some onion dip."

Before I got up, he grabbed my arm. "Would you relax? I'm not going to suckerfish myself to your lips just because you have beer breath." I smiled, resisting the impulse to make a joke about how disappointed I was. He seemed to know what I was thinking because he gave me an admonishing look. "Besides, wine was my preferred vice of choice, and vodka."

I abruptly burped and covered my mouth again. "I'm so sorry. I did not know that was in there."

His face contorted as he tried to control his laughter, but he failed miserably. "You know, Lenore, you are something else."

I uncovered my mouth, comfortable that all the air had been expelled. "You mean rude, unladylike, and a little disgusting?"

"Hmm, no, not the words I would have used. Perhaps audacious, independent, and... alluring."

"Alluring?" I laughed. If I hadn't just had two very quick beers, I might have flushed rather than laughed, but I wasn't as coy with beer in me. "Since when do you find me alluring? I thought I was repugnant to you."

He craned his head back and blinked at me, dumbfounded. "When have I ever given you that impression?"

I smiled, not wanting to tell him. I rolled my pursed lips around debating on what to tell him. "Well, alright, we've already hammered out my relationship issues with Garrett, your relationship issues with God, so we might as well tackle our relationship issues."

"*We* have relationship issues?" He tried to say it seriously, but he couldn't hold back the smile. "Pray, do tell of this soap opera I was too obtuse to notice."

"Don't be blithe with me, and it's not a soap opera, it's just an observation."

"What observation?" he asked, leaning closer to me.

I tried to hold his eyes, but this time I couldn't. I tried to keep my comedy up, but I couldn't. I could feel the situation turn serious and I was instantly regretting bringing it up.

"Is it because I turned you down after you kissed me?" he asked sympathetically.

"No, but that didn't help. It also didn't help that you practically slammed the door in my face to get me out of there."

"It was a confusing time for both of us. We needed to not be together. I explained all that then." I could hear the tone in his voice.

It was a chiding tone that said my feelings about the situation were inconsequential to his logic. Now I really didn't want to talk about it.

I shook my head to say as much, but he wasn't going to let it go. "I've always welcomed your visits, even though it was hard to tell since I just ranted and preached at you. How did you get the impression I find you repugnant? Lenore?" He touched my hand and I pulled it away.

"Don't, you'll make me cry. I'm sick of crying. Just let it go."

He sighed in frustration, but I knew he still wasn't going to let it go. "Now I really need to know. I've obviously offended you on a deeper level. I want you to tell me what I did. I can't even begin to understand how you could think I feel that way about you, especially after what I've told you."

I gritted my teeth trying to fight off the emotion I was feeling. If it wasn't for the beer I could have controlled them. Ironically, without the beer I would never have brought it up in the first place.

"Lenore," he whispered, seeing my discomfort, but still demanding the truth.

"Okay, just let me get control before I say it. Christ, you're a damned bloodhound for my pain." I turned my head so I didn't see his reaction to that statement. When I felt like I had a margin of control over my faculties, I looked back at him.

He was pained with guilt and he didn't even understand how he had slighted me. I was mortified that the significance of my comment had been blown way out of proportion. "You didn't do anything. *That* was what you did." I rolled my eyes at my own lame admission.

"I'm sorry, I don't understand."

It occurred to me that he didn't realize how his inaction looked from my perspective, so I tried to put it in terms he could understand. I leaned over and lowered my voice, though I kept my eyes on him so he would know I was saying it in earnest and not simply to be insulting.

"You fucked everything on two legs that walked into that church seeking your help... except me. You never even let your eyes sink below my neck." I could see the shock in his eyes, and I leaned back to watch the crowd while he let my words sink in. I couldn't keep the tears back any longer, but at least they were quiet unobtrusive ones and not wretched uncontrollable sobs.

For a long time, I waited for him to say something, anything, to make me feel better, but he didn't. I couldn't imagine how he had gone from being so compassionate to so cold, but I could only assume he didn't know how to say, *I'm just not that into you*, without hurting my feelings.

When his hand came before my face, I stared at it like it was a foreign object. I looked up to his face and I knew he was wordlessly requesting a dance. I debated whether to walk away and leave him with the cold silence he had just put me through, but being alone didn't sound any better than sitting in silence.

I pressed my hand into his and followed him to the dance floor. He pulled me close, closer than I thought he would. He pressed his temple to mine so his mouth was right next to my ear. "Can you hear me?" He spoke in a whisper, but we were so close I could hear him clearly.

I nodded and I felt him swallow hard.

"You are not repugnant to me. You have never been repugnant to me." He was censuring me and I pushed away, not willing to be reprimanded for feeling the way he made me feel. He pulled me in tighter. "Stay with me, please. I can't bear to look at you as I say this. As much as I want to, I can't. Will you stay and hear me out?"

I nodded and his grip relaxed. "I won't repeat my observations from before, but rest assured I do find you very alluring." I wanted to pull away again, simply because I wasn't interested in how alluring I was as His divine light. "Lenore, I want you to be happy, so I will do whatever I can to make that happen. I know you aren't aware of it, but Garrett has been watching you like a hawk all night."

This was not the conversation I expected to be having. He was right that I hadn't seen Garrett. I wasn't even entirely sure he was still around, but then again he was a stealthy bastard.

"This is going to make him intolerably jealous, and he'll cut in to get you away from me. I want you to let him."

"You really will do anything to get away from me," I snarled in his ear.

"Stop it!" he hissed. "It's agonizing for me to hear you say that. I can't even begin to defend myself. The way I feel about you..."

"You could just say you don't think of me that way, or you're not attracted to me. You don't have to try to pawn me off." My voice was strained with emotion, but I couldn't help but feel rejected on so many levels by a man who, by no exaggeration, had his own harem.

I could feel his grip tighten and wondered if he was angry or hurt. "Lenore, neither of those statements would be true. Please understand me, because I can't go through this conversation with you ever again. I can't be with you and I can't explain that, but please don't challenge my resolve, because I will lose against you."

Priest leaned back and I looked at his face, but he was already looking behind him. Garrett had come to interrupt, as Priest said he would. An offer of a partner exchange was made and Priest agreed.

Priest pulled away from me, and he only offered me a fleeting glance before he took Garrett's former partner in his arms. Garrett embraced me and I should have been happy, but I felt confused, rejected, and betwixt all at once. All I could do was lean on Garrett and hope I could find comfort there, because I apparently wasn't going to find it with Priest.

Just to Clarify

DEVIN DUTIFULLY CARED FOR Haden, drawing her into his arms and carrying her into the house. I slipped out of the SUV still in a haze. Garrett didn't understand my quiet disregard for reality, but he did glean that I needed to be home. To add insult to injury, Priest had brought Garrett's former friend home. She apparently didn't care who she went home with as long as she got with someone.

We stepped inside the side door to the kitchen and there was a quick conversation about who would take what rooms. Garrett had invited himself into mine for the night, and offered August's old room to Priest. I wanted to scream and yell and throw break-ables in a tantrum to end all tantrums, but I couldn't figure out a way to do that and still maintain what little hold I had on my sanity. It was such a tenuous thread now as it was.

Garrett pulled me along to my room and locked the door be-hind me. I felt stifled despite being in the comfort of my wide room. He looked me over, trying to figure out what was wrong with me. When no obvious answer came, he kissed me.

It was a gentle kiss, but one with increasing meaning. *I'm sorry. Are you okay? Forgive me. I forgive you. I want you.* When it was clear I wasn't going to participate he pulled away. He looked disappointed, but he kissed my forehead and took a step back.

"Do you want me to go?"

I shook my head. I didn't want to be alone. Even if he wasn't the right someone, at least he was someone. At this point, I was in no condition to judge who was right or wrong for me anyhow.

"Do you want to sleep?"

I nodded. I wanted to make this night go away as fast as possible.

"Do you want to change?"

I looked down at my blue sweater and jeans. I nodded again. I cleared my throat and shook away my ridiculous catatonic state. "I need to brush my teeth."

He nodded this time. He seemed relieved that I was talking, but also a little apprehensive about me leaving the room. It was a reasonable concern, given my history of fleeing from my problems. Little did he know, I had nowhere else to go.

I slipped out of the room, shutting the door behind me. I could see a light from under August's door, and I heard Jimmy the Card starting his lovemaking hour from inside. I wanted to throw up, and since I was already heading to the bathroom I made my teeth brushing worth it.

Six heaves later and I was thoroughly cleaned out. I had only had two beers but the quick succession was not a good idea, even if it was sacrilege to waste our supply. I flushed the toilet and rinsed out my mouth before grabbing my toothbrush and paste out of my drawer.

I noted the old box of tampons in my drawer, and scoffed. I had imagined one day my cycle would come back, but like the other women of the post-apocalyptic world, I was barren. It was a relief to some like Haden who preferred not to endure motherhood, but to me it was a reminder that this was not simply a natural disaster we could recover from. This was the end of days, and not a single new soul would be allowed onto this Earth.

I brushed my teeth with the devotion of a little kid not wanting to go to bed. Each crevice and nook was scrubbed to a fine sheen. When I finally spat the last of the toothpaste out and turned to vacate my short sanctuary, Priest was standing in the door.

His shirt was off and his pajama bottoms hung just under his hip bone. I averted my eyes to avoid seeing what he had to offer below that deep waistline. He was like a walking advertisement of what I couldn't have.

I caught his eyes and I knew I was burning a hole right through his. He looked guilty and yet resolute, like he wouldn't concede to offer me anything more than what he already had. "Is that it then?" I nodded to August's room. "You're not even cowering behind your vow of celibacy."

"I won't have this conversation with you. You know how I feel. Let that be enough."

"I don't know how you feel," I stated clearly. "I know of your attraction. I know of your blockade on it, but I do not know how you *feel*."

"I thought that was obvious," he said.

"Lenore?" Garrett said from the door of my room. "You coming to bed?"

I resisted the urge to look at Priest for that answer, and nodded. "Yeah, I am." I started to move forward, but Priest didn't move right away. When he finally did, he only angled himself enough so I could get by.

"Good night, Lenore," he mumbled as I slipped past him. "I love you." He said it casually like it was something we had said to each other a hundred times in passing, but it wasn't. That was a new statement. That was the answer to my question.

All new emotions piled up on top of the old ones, and I could do nothing, because Priest was already shutting the door to the bathroom and Garrett was standing in my doorway waiting for me to join him.

Sweet Revenge

I WAS NO LONGER confused. I understood the situation perfectly now. Priest was in love with me, and because of that love, he couldn't let himself have me. He was willing to defile his vows with women he didn't love, but not me. It was all very noble, until you looked at it from my perspective.

I was quickly falling in love—or perhaps had already fallen in love—with a man I could talk to, laugh with, and trust with my life, but he wouldn't touch me with a ten-foot pole. Yes, from my perspective this really just sucked.

The anger I felt was beyond words, but it wasn't beyond action. I ripped off my sweater and pants. Garrett was about to ask something, probably involving pajamas, but I muffled his attempts to communicate with a hard kiss. He was surprised by it, but he didn't hesitate to respond. That's what I liked about Garrett. He was never going to push me away. He was always willing to give me what I wanted, at least in the bedroom.

I pushed him toward the bed, and he resisted only long enough to get his clothes off. I pushed against him to get him onto the bed, but he wouldn't budge. Instead he lifted me and set me on the bed gently.

I reached to pull him back when he pulled away, but he pressed his hand on my chest and pushed me back down.

"Lenore, slow down, I'm not going anywhere." He sat beside me on the bed and leaned in for a less aggressive kiss. "Not that I don't appreciate the enthusiasm, but what changed your mind?"

He kissed my breasts through my bra, provoking my nipples into attentiveness. I relaxed back, remembering how capable he was with my body. He was still waiting for an answer when I looked back up at him. I smiled and shrugged. "I figured I better get while the getting's good."

"The getting's very good." He trailed kisses down my stomach and I arched to receive them.

"You'll be here in the morning?" I asked even though I probably wouldn't have stopped him if he said no.

"Yes, I promise," he said, sliding his fingers into my panties. I groaned loudly to let him know I was enjoying it, but more importantly to let Priest know I was enjoying it, in case he was listening. "What shall I train you in this evening?" He teased with words while he teased me with his fingers.

"Anything, just don't stop. And don't leave," I added in case my fear of being alone wasn't already my most notable personality trait.

"I won't. Just lie back and let me make you moan again. And don't be shy about it. I don't mind letting everyone in this house know that I can make up for any pain I've caused you, and then some." I didn't smile, because he wasn't kidding, and with the attentions he paid me the remainder of the night, I had to remind myself I wasn't seeking revenge against the whole house.

The Morning After

IT DIDN'T SURPRISE ME to see Devin and Haden still in bed. She was pretty messed up, and I heard her puking early in the morning. I was certain Devin was right by her side holding her hair back like the dutiful man he was. August's door was open and the bed was freshly made sans overnight guest.

I crept downstairs and waited on the steps to hear if she was still around. I could see from the reflection in the 70s-style sunburst wall mirror at the base of the stairs that the only people in the kitchen were Priest and Garrett. Priest was sitting down to a cup of coffee, reading his book. Garrett poured himself a fresh cup and leaned against the counter. He had a watchful eye on Priest.

Priest looked up from his book, no doubt sensing the less-than-friendly observation. "Something I can help you with, Garrett?" he asked, hiding his irritation rather well. I was about to get up so I could break up any minor disputes, but then Garrett spoke.

"I was wondering what your intentions are with Lenore." I froze, shocked by the question. Priest must have been just as surprised because he didn't move for several seconds. He just stared at him.

"Excuse me?" He folded his book around his mark and set it off to the side.

"August didn't approve of her friendship with you."

Priest tented his hands over the table before responding. "I didn't disagree with that, and neither did Lenore."

"Yet here you are."

"I've come to offer my condolences to my friend."

"You two had some very heated and emotional discussions last night." Priest didn't say anything. "I don't want to see Lenore get hurt."

Priest's chair squawked as he pushed away from the table. "I was under the impression you enjoyed hurting her." He must have changed positions in case the conversation turned physical. Garrett didn't initiate anything, but the two men stared each other down from their respective corners. The tension was palpable even from my position on the stairs.

"Lenore is a good deal stronger than any of you give her credit for," Garrett said when his temper no longer hampered his verbal skills. "I've seen what she can do, because I've trained her to do it. You can balk at those scars as much as you want, but she can't meet her potential if all of you keep treating her like a damned porcelain doll."

Garrett pulled out the chair across from Priest and sat down. I thought he might have done it as a peace offering. Garrett wasn't likely to sit during an argument unless he honestly wanted to keep things civil. "I'm here to make sure Lenore gets back on track. My concern is you will be a distraction. What are your intentions?" he asked again.

"What is this interrogation really about, Garrett? Possession? Do you want me out of the picture?"

"Yeah, I do. Ideally I'd like everyone out of the picture, but I know Devin's got her under lock and key, and I'm not so sure Haden wouldn't put a bullet in me if I tried to take off with her. So, to answer your question, this interrogation is about whose side you're on."

"I'm on Lenore's side."

"She isn't a side, she's an outcome. Matthew, the first time I came after her, she ran to you. You convinced her to keep going with the training."

"I didn't convince her of anything, it was her choice. However, I never would have let her go if I had known what you were going to put her through."

"Stop focusing on the pain, Matthew. Each one of those scars is a lesson learned. I need to know what you will say to her this time when she comes to you crying, bleeding, and wanting to stop."

"You're going to put her through the same torture?"

Garrett ignored his question. He was done listening to pandering sympathy. "If you want her to succeed you have to kiss her boo-boos and send her right back out to fight again, like you did before. Do you understand?"

"She didn't continue training because of me. The only reason she went back to you was because of August. She was abjectly devoted to your sister."

"We all were. My sister was a born leader and I respected her objectives even when I thought she was wrong, but she wasn't wrong about Lenore. I know that now. My sister knew she was going to die. I think she hoped Lenore would be able to save her, but... sometimes the dead bring us more motivation than the living. Lenore will continue to fight in my sister's name. How hard will depend on you and the others."

Priest looked down at his coffee cup. "You want me to watch you beat the hell out of her, and not do anything to stop it?"

"If you can't do it, then leave. She'll try to stay strong in front of the others, but I know she won't be able to for you. If you really want to help Lenore, you have to be strong enough to push her back to me when she comes running to you." I wondered if Priest found as much irony in that statement as I did.

"Okay," was all he said.

Refresher Course

"**Y**OU READY?" DEVIN BRACED himself, prepared to attack me.

"Don't ask her if she's ready," Garrett griped. "Grim don't ask if you're ready before they attack." He paced on the sidelines of the snowy lawn. Priest was getting a lesson about guns from Haden. I wasn't sure if he intended to carry one, or if he just wanted something to do with his time. Or perhaps he was looking for a reason to be outside so he could watch my lesson.

Haden and Devin agreed to take him on easier than I thought. They might have been too stunned about August's death to deny a new ally, or they might have realized he wasn't such a vile man when he was sober.

Devin dove at me, and I jumped out of the way. Garrett scoffed in disgust. "Well, don't just stand there, go after her again. For the love of... just let me do it!"

"No!" Devin yelled. "You aren't touching her again."

"Lenore!" Garrett put enough demand in my name to make me jump. "Take him down, now!"

I didn't want to for a good number of reasons. One, I hated to show up Devin. He was such a good fighter, but he was severely underestimating my level. Two, I hated to hurt him. He was currently my perfect platonic lover and it pained me to do him harm. And third, I didn't want to listen to Garrett.

His conversation with Priest yesterday morning was still irking me. He shouldn't have asked Priest to plot against me. What annoyed me the most, though, was that Priest agreed to it.

I roundhouse-kicked Devin in the face. While he was still stunned, I buckled his knees and punched him low in the back. He grunted and fell to the ground holding his back. When I came to check on him he put up his hands in surrender.

I genuflected some distance from him and offered him my guilty sympathy. "Please, don't make me hurt you, Devin. Just let Garrett do it. I like hurting him."

"I don't want to see you get hurt," he mumbled into the snow.

"I don't want to see *you* get hurt," I whispered.

"Oh, this is craptastic!" Garrett griped behind Devin. "Will you just let me do this? She can handle it! You two are too damn gushy for real fighting."

Devin rolled over and looked at him. "You're a sadist!"

"I'm a realist. Please, release your umbilical cord so we can move on with this." Garrett was at his limit on civility—if Devin didn't give him permission he was going to dive in anyway.

"Fine, you can—"

Garrett didn't wait for any further information. He lunged at me. Still crouched by Devin I leapt out of his range and rolled to a standing position. Naturally, he didn't wait for my recovery and I was dodging punches left and right.

He grabbed my neck, but I twisted away, elbowing him in the face. He kicked my calves out, sending me to my knees. I took advantage of the position and elbowed his crotch. He grimaced, but fell on top of me. His knee dug into my back and shoved my head into the ground.

"Dead," he announced when it was clear that flopping like a fish was not a tactical maneuver. "Again." He pulled himself off of me and I got back up to start over again. "What was your mistake?" he asked as he walked away.

I looked to Devin who was impressed by my effort even though I lost. I could tell he was having mixed feelings about this. He could see I did know what I was doing, but he could also see there were no safe words for this game, because it wasn't a game.

"Lenore?" Punctuated with the scolding question mark. *Damn him.*

"I should have rolled away from you instead of taking the crotch shot. An enemy in reach is dangerous even if they're in pain." I felt like I was back in kindergarten.

"Not to mention, you might want me intact for later tonight," he mumbled and winked at me.

Wow, Garrett Smith joking and flirting. Was this my lucky day? I dodged his incoming attack and slammed my fist into his back on the way by.

Probably not.

Notes in Study Hall

I LIMPED INTO THE living room with my pajamas on and a first aid kit in hand. I had missed supper in lieu of a very hot bath, but I had a few scrapes to have assessed. When I stepped into the living room I got four different looks.

Holy shit you look terrible, courtesy of my girl power sister on the couch. I noted it was now three against two with the males in the lead. I had always preferred three against one, with Devin on the losing end, although I don't imagine he ever considered it the losing end, since he got to be adored by three women.

Devin, on the other hand, looked on me with solemn guilt and sympathy. He stood up when I entered the room. "You want some supper?" I nodded and he went to fetch me a plate.

Priest was also on the couch, looking me over with the same guilt, but without the sympathy. He seemed almost angry, like he couldn't believe I was doing this to myself. He looked at the box in my hand and started to say something.

"Come here, Lenore," Garrett said from his chair by the fire. Priest glanced at him and didn't say whatever he intended to say. "Come on," he said again when I hesitated.

I kind of felt like a dog being called to my owner, but there was a protocol to follow. I stood in front of Garrett and he pushed, prodded, and poked at me, finding a bruised rib and a sliver of a branch in my back I hadn't even realized was there.

I sat at Garrett's feet and let him tend to my back, dabbing it with disinfectant and salve. When Devin brought me my supper, I thanked him. He eyed Garrett and persisted to give me a kiss on the lips. He kept it fairly chaste, but he just wanted to make a point.

Considering I was back to being a punching bag, it really didn't matter who peed on me at this point. So long as I had food to eat and someone to pull the branches out of my back, I was good. At least for now.

Garrett brushed my wet hair behind my ear and dabbed ointment on a cut above my eyebrow. Now that we had slept together, several times, he tended to my injuries differently. He was gentle and almost sensual about it. I hoped it wasn't just for show. I hoped he really did care about me.

I looked up at him to see what his expression was. It was impassive, as usual. He caught my eye, and furrowed his brow. "What?" he asked.

"Do you like me?" I whispered so no one else could hear me.

He looked me over and smiled. A rare treat indeed. "Yeah, I like you just fine."

I pulled my shirt down to cover my back, and settled against his knees with my head rested on his leg. He finished tending to the cut above my eye, after which he ran his fingers through my hair a few times before getting back to his magazine.

I watched the fire so I couldn't see Priest. I wanted to know what he thought of Garrett's healing ministrations. Was he jealous or was he happy to be rid of me? Either way, I wasn't going to be satisfied, so I just didn't look at him.

Relationships Suck

"Again," Garrett directed. It was his favorite word, but it was fast becoming my least favorite.

I threw my next knife at the target as he directed. Every cutlery blade in the kitchen was at my disposal, but none of them had managed to stick to the garden shed, let alone hit the red target Garrett had painted on it. Just like all the others, the knife hilt hit the wall, chipping off white paint before landing harmlessly in the snow.

"Don't try to spin the knife." He suffused himself to me, directing me like a tennis instructor explaining a backhand. "Don't think of it like a circus trick. Think of it like throwing darts. You want to arch the blade from this skyward position, to a forward position so it will stick in the wood." He used my arm to demonstrate his description. "First establish how to get the point in wood, and we can work on aim later."

I repeated the movement a few times before throwing the next knife. It didn't feel quite as flashy his way, but I managed to get the blade to hit the wood instead of the hilt. It didn't stay there, but it was progress. I looked back at Garrett for encouragement, but he just handed me another knife.

I threw it again with a bit more zeal, but it curved too far and the hilt hit. I sighed, grabbing another knife before Garrett could tell me to. I was happy to be taking a break from combat, but knife throwing seemed like a useless skill to me. Garrett was preparing me for the tournament finale more than any real-world battle.

I threw the knife again rather half-heartedly, and it stuck. "Ooh!" I raised my hands in triumph, but the blade slipped and fell to the ground. "Oh." I lowered my hands.

Garrett chuckled behind me and moved up close behind me again. "The problem is your consistency, Lenore. After you get comfortable with this distance we can adjust, just like you would adjust to throw a ball harder if the catcher was farther away. You have to start and release at the same spot each time. Let's just work with the steak knives since they're all the same size and weight. Don't worry about embedding the tip. I'm happy if you chip the paint with the blade."

I looked at him over my shoulder. He had a slight smile on his face. I wanted him to tell me I was doing well, so I knew this wasn't a waste of his time, but I wasn't sure how to ask for that. "Can you do this?" I tapped the blade of one of the steak knives in my palm.

He perked an eyebrow as if I had just double-dog dared him. I turned around and put the knife in his hand. "Show me." I smirked.

"You're supposed to be training, not me," he said firmly, but I could see a slight amusement in his eyes, even if it didn't reach his lips.

"Those who can't do, teach." I crossed my arms, this time making it obvious that I was double-dog daring him.

He rolled his eyes, but I could see he was struggling to keep his smile at bay. He brushed me aside and moved into position. In quick succession, he threw all the remaining knives with perfect form. When he got to the large chef's knife, he flipped it around and threw it by the blade. I could only assume the weight was too heavy to hope for a gentle arch.

When he was finished, the shed looked like a knife block. Garrett turned to me with mock annoyance, holding his hands on his hips. "There. Can we move on with your lesson? As you can see, I am perfectly qualified to be teaching you."

"Don't give me that tone." I put my hands on my hips as well. "I know you enjoyed that."

He looked me over and shook his head slightly. "I don't like showing off. It's unnecessary, and it doesn't help you." He moved to the shed to collect the knives. I followed right after him.

"Actually it does," I said matter-of-factly. He glanced back at me, looking for clarification. "I need to see your form. I'm a visual learner. Jumping in and doing it doesn't necessarily speed up my understanding, it just confuses me. I do better if you show me how to do it first."

Garrett stopped before the shed and turned around. He looked confused. "You're just telling me this now?"

"Well, it doesn't apply to all situations. I mean, treading water is still jumping in the pool and not drowning. But the breast stroke? Well, that I would need to observe first."

He laughed and shook his head. "That explains a lot, Lenore. I wish you would have told me this eight months ago."

I ripped one of the knives out of the shed wall. "Eight months ago your version of training was sticking this chef's knife to my throat."

"That was your treading water lesson, and you did very well."

"Yeah, well, fear is an amazing motivator—but of course there are other ways to motivate." I pulled another knife out while he gathered my fallen ones.

"Such as?"

"For starters, you could tell me when I'm doing a good job. I am a human being, you know. With, like, feelings and stuff." I widened my eyes and mouth at the shocking revelation and headed back to my throwing line.

"I know that, Lenore. You know why I'm hard on you."

"I know why you think you need to be hard on me, but yes, Garrett, I understand the method in your madness, and I'm not going to run away, no matter how mean you are to me." I added the last part with childish undertone. He paused, noting it, but didn't say anything. He stabbed the knives into the wood sawhorse in front of me that marked my place and watched my form.

"Why did you ask me last night if I liked you?" he asked on my first throw. The knife went well off the target and bounced into the bushes. I would have blamed it on his sudden interest in my question, but I think it was just a bad throw.

"I was just curious." He pulled out a knife and handed it to me, observing my lack of eye contact carefully. "You treat me like a project sometimes. I wondered how much of this," I motioned between us, "is the result of close proximity and shared pain." I threw the knife and for once it stuck, but the conversation was beyond my growing talents now.

"I've always been very frank with you about what I can and cannot offer you. You know I have obligations in Chicago."

"Does that mean when you're done here, you'll be leaving again?"

"Yes, but that's nothing new."

"Maybe we shouldn't be doing this," I said before I thought about what I wanted his answer to be. I stuck the knife again. Naturally, I was doing well now that I was distracted by the drama of my sex life.

"What, training or fucking?"

I would have preferred if he didn't refer to what we were doing with such vulgar terminology, but he wasn't wrong. It certainly wasn't making love. "It's kind of messed up, don't you think? I mean you and me. We beat up on each other and then go have sex. That's probably unhealthy, right?"

"Lenore, every intimacy we've shared has been instigated by you, and you haven't exactly been kicking me out of your bed at night."

I frowned and threw three more successful throws. Garrett finally took note of my triumph as well as my increasing accuracy. He handed me three more knives. "Now you know why I asked you that question last night. I know you want to train me." Bullseye hit with the steak knife. "I know you enjoy sex with me." Bullseye with the paring knife, but it didn't stick—too light. "But do you even give a shit about me beyond punching me in the face or sticking your dick in me?"

The last knife was the chef's knife. I flipped it around as Garrett had. I didn't get a bullseye, but it embedded nicely into the wall of the shed. I turned to him and waited for an answer.

He sighed and looked over to the shed before returning his attention to me. "What do you want me to do, Lenore? I can't stay with you. I can't in good conscious offer you the sweet sensitive man you want and then walk away. That seems cruel to me. I thought we were enjoying the time we have together. If you're developing feelings for me..." He winced like he hated to finish that sentence.

"Developing?" I snapped. The lesson was over, or would be very soon. I faced off his piteous sympathy with an independence that could only be learned at the hands of life's many disappointments. "Of course I have feelings for you, you glacial son of a bitch. Do you think I would have given myself to you if I thought as little of it as crossing the street?

"Feelings! Fuck you, Garrett! I'm not asking you to propose to me. I just want a little respect and compassion that isn't subsequent to an orgasm. I know it's in there somewhere, I've seen it once or twice."

Garrett shifted uncomfortably, but didn't offer any defense, which wasn't a surprise, since it would involve verbalizing his *feelings!*

"This lesson is over. I think I've got the hang of it. I'll practice on my own from here on out." I stomped off, vindicated by my response to his frigid behavior, but I already knew I wouldn't feel that way tonight in my cold bed.

Just Friends

"MAY I SIT WITH you?" Priest asked like the couch had suddenly become sovereign territory to my ass. Everyone else was still eating supper. I wasn't hungry, partially because Garrett hadn't made any effort to apologize for being a heartless ass, and I didn't want to stare across the table at him while he didn't stare back.

"No, I demand all my subjects kneel in my presence." I motioned to the floor before me. Priest stared at me and I snickered. "Crap, just sit, Priest."

He sat down beside me with one arm behind me, but not touching me. "Are you ever going to call me by my birth name?" He crossed his leg and I could see holes in his jeans at the knee.

"You've been doing too much praying." I tickled his bare knee with my fingernail. He moved his knee away, but smiled at me. "At least I hope that's what you're doing on your knees." I offered him an unabashed look of shock and he grinned at my joke.

"I don't keep my pants on when—" He stopped mid-sentence and his face went ashen like he might be sick. He cleared his throat. "I've been praying a little more lately, but not like I used to and not for the same reasons." He fiddled with the metal cross I made him. I was surprised he hadn't given himself tetanus as much as he rubbed at it.

"I don't know whether to tell you that's good or bad. I'm not sure where you're at right now."

"I don't want to make you uncomfortable."

I nodded. I didn't want to be uncomfortable either. If I was a good friend, I might have told him to share his trials with his religious path with me, but since he told me I was his only connection to his once devote life, it kind of made my sympathetic ear go instantly deaf.

"How are things going? You seem to be on the outs with Garrett. Has he hurt you?" I looked away. There weren't any safe conversations left for me and Priest. "It's none of my business; I just want to make sure you're okay."

"And if I'm not?" I whispered, hoping the answer to that question wasn't a dead stare, but it was. I sighed and looked away. "This is so hard, Priest."

"I know. I'm sorry. If you want me to leave, I will."

"No, that's not what I want either. I think I just want to erase my memory and go back to being blissfully ignorant of what I'm missing out on."

"Please, let me bless you," he whispered abruptly and reached for my head.

I pulled away from his hand and glared at him in disgust. "What the hell? I seriously don't get men today."

"Lenore," he pleaded. I wondered if his blessings on me had become a sick compulsion.

"No, just let it go, Priest. I don't understand this connection between me and Him in your eyes, but that's your issue to work through, not mine. I have to save the world, or at least part of it. My plate is already full and I didn't save room for bat-shit crazy dessert."

Priest's eyes fell as I finished my inconsiderate statement. It took me a moment before I realized I had broken my promise to him. I winced, feeling the guilt of my smart-ass comment. "Priest," I murmured, but he was already up and walking out of the front/back door. "Shit," I hissed, bashing my palms into my forehead.

"Everything okay?" Devin asked from the kitchen table when I got up to go after him.

"No, I've been hanging out with Garrett too much. His asinine behavior is contagious."

Devin snorted and Haden hid a smile. I couldn't see what expression Garrett was giving me, but I didn't stop to find out.

I stepped out onto the porch and found Priest standing by the steps looking out onto the vast nothingness of what was once a cornfield. The vacant land had already developed straggly cedar trees and waist-deep wild grasses.

I took a deep breath and let it out slowly as I leaned my head against his back between his shoulder blades. "I'm sorry. I said I would never make that reference again. I was being a smart-ass, and I let my mouth ramble. You may have observed my handy talent for foot-in-mouth disease."

He didn't say anything. I groaned in frustration and gripped his arm.

"Please, Priest, I can't bear having you mad at me. Your disappointment in me is worse than Devin's puppy dog face." He still didn't speak. I wasn't even sure if he was angry or hurt. "Please, Matthew." I tested his name out on my lips, and I immediately knew why I didn't want to say his real name. It felt too good, too intimate.

He turned around and looked at me. He still looked mad, but I could see he enjoyed hearing me say his name for once. "Let me bless you." It wasn't a question like he often posed his requests. It was an outright demand.

I rolled my eyes and was about to acquiesce, but he interrupted me.

"And how is your eye roll any different from the words you just hurt me with?"

I was on a streak tonight. If I could finish the day by kicking a puppy, I would have exceeded my own personal best. "Sorry." I held my hands up in surrender. "I'll let you bless me."

"No, I want you to accept my blessing." I shook my head and shrugged. I wasn't seeing the difference. "I want you to open your mind and your heart to me, and let me offer you God's love." I wasn't aware I was stepping backward until he grabbed me and pulled me back to him. I was instantly shaking and it wasn't from the cold.

"Why does that scare you so much?"

"I don't know, it sounds like you're asking to brainwash me."

"Okay." He nodded and positioned me between him and the pole. My claustrophobia flared. "How about this? You open your mind and heart to me and I'll give you my love." I froze, remembering his admission a few nights ago. "Does that sound better to you?"

"Yeah, but only cause your making it sound really hot." I smiled brightly to take the tension of my body, but it didn't work.

He luckily smiled back so I didn't have to feel stupid. "It does sound hot, doesn't it? Well, I can't offer you an orgasm, at least not one I'm present for." I chuckled at his joke, even though I was about to hyperventilate. "But I can offer you this."

He leaned in, touching his forehead to mine and taking my face in his hands. Instinctively, I put my hands over his. I wanted to rip them off and run away, and yet I didn't. "Why am I terrified of you right now?" I panted.

"You aren't terrified. You're anxious. You have a sense for people, Lenore. You can read them, but you're not fully in tune with that ability yet. Not the way I am. Not the way I hope one day I can be." I could feel him shift like he wanted to kiss me, but he moved away again.

"I've had a lot of time to think. I'm not entirely sure about a lot of things, but I do know one thing. I'm not crazy." He started his litany. It was hypnotic, and I let myself relax as best I could with him.

When I relaxed, his words changed. They were all foreign, but I did get the sense they were good words, words that would help me and not hurt me. With that knowledge, I let go fully and opened my mind and heart as best I could without actually understanding how exactly to do that. Essentially, I just told my own thoughts and feelings to shut the hell up.

It wasn't long after I felt a welling of emotions not unlike my prior cathartic experience with him. This time, however, it wasn't solely my pain building to climax. It was my anger, my fear, my love, and desires. You name it, I was feeling it to a height of mental breakdown proportions. The peak of this emotional journey was too much to fathom in my own mind, let alone articulate outside of it. I couldn't verbalize it, so I tried to simply react to it.

The screaming probably wasn't necessary, but I was really freaked out.

Family

T HE SCREAMING WASN'T NECESSARY, but the vomiting was. Apparently, feeling every emotion possible, to a pinnacle height, was not unlike riding a roller coaster after a Thanksgiving dinner.

At some point, the door slammed open and mass hysteria broke out. Haden was holding my hair back while I puked, as any good female friend would. Someone had slammed Priest up against the house. Judging by the shoes I was seeing from the view between my shaking legs, I guessed Devin. Garrett was standing to one side asking a laundry list of questions that Priest wasn't answering. He wasn't answering Devin's questions either.

When I was done expelling my last meal, I returned to an upright position, letting Haden hold me steady. Priest was watching me intently. Waiting to see if I was okay? Gauging my reaction to whatever the hell he just did to me?

Garrett gave me a questioning once-over, but seemed to decide I wasn't hurt. Devin looked between me and Priest to determine if what had just transpired was violent, sexual, or other. Considering I couldn't even answer that and I had been there, he was justifiably infuriated by our lack of responses.

While the men stumbled into baffled silence, Haden had no trouble verbalizing her frustrations. "What the fuck just happened out here?" She scanned me, then Priest. "What did you do to her?" Priest didn't answer. I got the impression they could have threatened to beat him to a pulp and he still wouldn't have told them. It was possible he didn't know either.

I put my hands up in surrender. "I may or may not have over-reacted."

"To what? What did he do?" Haden's voice pitched.

I opened my mouth to provide an answer, but I didn't have one. Priest didn't offer any reason for me not to speak, but I also didn't feel comfortable sharing what I had experienced. I was certain it wasn't meant to harm me, but I wasn't sure if I approved of what had happened either.

My emotional life had flashed before my mind. Was that the blessing Priest spoke of, or was it more? Was it, as he said, his love... or was it His love? In either case, I really needed to look up the definition of love, because what he had done felt more like a deep-tissue massage of my brain.

"Lenore?" Devin asked. His voice sounded concerned, but he was getting impatient.

"I'm fine." I checked my watch. "I'll take first watch. I'm clearly having an overly dramatic day, so I should stay out here to cool off."

Devin released Priest and shifted to stand in front of me. "Are you shitting me? You're not going to tell me?" He must have felt betrayed, because he didn't even wait for a feeble stuttered answer to pop out of my gaping mouth before he stormed off.

"Shit." I looked at Haden. She was just as angry, but the look on her face was a rebuke. I imagine it was the same look August would have given me. "I don't know. Ask him." It was probably a little late to throw Priest under the bus, but I was desperate to avoid having everyone pissed off at me again.

Haden threw a glare at Priest. He didn't take his eyes off me when he answered. "I think it's best we chock this night up to a lot of emotions in a very small house. Wasn't there a discussion about getting a bigger house?"

"Yeah, right." Haden crossed her arms and stepped between Priest and me. It seemed to be a protective stance, but I think she just wanted to draw Priest's attention. "Like this is a long-term commitment for either of you."

Priest finally took his eyes off me and looked at Haden. He was bewildered by her accusation. He looked to Garrett, who wasn't daunted by her comment. "I'm here for Lenore." Priest glanced back at me as if the comment had come directly from me.

Haden applauded him. "Congratulations, way to sober up and get on board after all the hard knocks have been taken. This team didn't need you before, and it doesn't need you now. The only reason you're here is because Lenore has a soft spot for strays and because you're on the safe side of sober."

I could see Priest tense with the chastising, but he took his medicine like a good boy.

"And you!" Haden shook her finger at Garrett.

"What about me?" he snarled.

"Your invite to this party is wearing out quicker than you might think."

"I'm here to train Lenore!" Garrett barked, no doubt offended that he had been lumped in with Priest as a hitchhiker to the team.

"Bullshit! She's trained. This is all just practice and extra skills she can learn with us. And for what? We don't even have a plan."

"August wanted her to compete—"

"Yes, but for what purpose? Her plots and plans were so goddamn ambiguous we might be preparing for a battle that has nothing to do with the tournaments. In the meantime we'll be endangering our lives every time we go back there. We have no freaking clue what we're doing and you're soothing all that panic with training, training, and more training. Did August ever enlighten you to her ultimate plan?"

I looked to Garrett. I hoped he might have an answer. He didn't, of course. No one did. August ran on instinct, the way she was teaching me to. She had a general understanding of the road that lay ahead, but pit stops were decided on an as-needed basis.

The road led her here. I was a pit stop.

At least, I *hope* I was a pit stop. She was starting to make me feel like the destination. Given that she was now gone and had passed her torch... err... car keys over to me, I couldn't help but wonder if I *was* her destination. If so, where the hell was *I* going? Was I supposed to be getting a road map with this heir to the hero shit?

"August didn't always know why she did things," Garrett clarified.

"So, we're all still in the same boat. But just to be clear, that boat is ours. Our captain may have died, but we are still her crew, and you two, as far as I'm concerned, are stowaways." Haden pointed a finger at each of them.

"So, you," Haden pinpointed Priest. "Keep your head down and your preaching to yourself, cause nobody cares about that crap anymore."

"And you," Haden turned her finger on Garrett who stiffened as if he wanted to slap it away. I was curious if Haden specifically pissed him off, or if he didn't take any criticism well. "You are not your sister. Don't think for one second that any of her title or position transfers to you."

Haden turned back around to me. "And you!" My eyes widened and I stepped back. I should have known I wasn't going to escape her admonishments. "You aren't August either. You'd better not start giving us inscrutable explanations. If you got a bad feeling about somebody or something, say so. Trust that we'll back you up. Understand?" She wasn't mad anymore, she was merely taking the opportunity to mention something she had on her mind.

I nodded. "Okay."

She waved her finger between Priest, me, and the remnants of my last meal. "I don't know what this was, and I don't want to know. You're safe. No one's possessed. I'm walking away."

Haden offered a look to each man before she headed to the door. Garrett didn't leave her room to move past him without her having to turn. Instead of squirming around him she stopped and waited for him to give her passage. "I am still armed, you cocky son of a bitch. Don't think I won't shoot you in the ass to prove a point."

He still didn't move. I could see him debating whether he wanted to take her down a peg by pinning her to the wall with brute strength.

"Garrett," I said quietly. He looked up at me, still holding the intensity in his eyes he intended for Haden. "Devin's already on a hair trigger. Don't mess with his girl."

When he still didn't move, I could feel the tension rise. They were two dogs about to fight. I rolled my eyes and grabbed the rifle leaning on the post near me. We had it stashed on the porch for emergencies. This wasn't exactly an emergency, but assholes probably counted too.

"Or we could skip Haden's ass shot, and go straight for the face." I aimed it right at his face, but didn't place my finger near the trigger, in case he would think I was serious.

He reached out, making Haden grasp for the gun holstered under her arm. He pulled open the screen door, and reached back to pop the knob to the inside door. "Excuse me, after you."

Haden must have questioned the gesture, but he played the gentleman well enough when he wanted to, it was hard to tell if he was being sincere or just mocking us. Either way he was probably doing it to assert his dominance, just in a different way.

She went inside, and Garrett paused, looking at me. "You mind if we chat after your watch?"

"Sure," I answered as I realized I was still holding the rifle on him. I grimaced and put it down against the post again. He slipped inside, closing the screen door behind him, but not the inside door. I looked at Priest. He took in a deep breath to say something, but I cut him off. "Goodnight, Priest. Thank you for yet another insightful yet inexplicable evening."

"I take it you don't want to talk about it."

"Nope." I did want to talk about it, but not at that moment. He nodded and headed inside, shutting both doors behind him.

Monkey Business

R ELIEVED OF MY POST, I headed upstairs to my room. I found Garrett curled up on my bed, napping. He must have suspected I would go out of my way not to talk to him. I was tempted to slip over to Priest's room—August's old room—and tap on his door. I would have preferred to talk to him about his extended blessing than talk to Garrett about relationship issues.

I knew Garrett could be a good man, but for some reason when we were around other people, he put up a wall between us. The only time he opened up and relaxed with me was when we were alone. That was fine and dandy for us, but from everyone else's perspective, I was sleeping with an asshole.

I was glad Haden said what she did to him and to all of us. I needed to know the dynamic of our group had not changed. I needed to know *I* still had a say in my life. Everything was not preset or predestined just because August said it was. What happened from here on out was up to us—the *three* of us.

Garrett stirred as I dressed for bed. I kept the door open for an easy escape. Priest and Haden were in their rooms, and Devin was outside, so propriety was no issue. He mumbled some kind of acknowledgment that no doubt sounded enunciated in his head. I ignored him and slipped on my ugliest pajama bottoms and my comfy frumpy sweatshirt. I wasn't interested in impressing him tonight.

He watched me intently as if he were evaluating the challenge before him—deciding if the fight was worth it.

"You said you wanted to talk, so talk," I said, putting on a little more deodorant since I had skipped over my shower for the night in lieu of sleep. My brain was far more sullied than my body anyway.

"I said I wanted to chat. That involves two people speaking."

"Depends which two," I mumbled.

Garrett climbed off the bed and shut my bedroom door, effectively blocking my escape. The amusing part was, he knew I had left it open for a quick exit, because he taught me to, and I knew he was closing it for the opposite reason, because he taught me that too. I moved to the back of the room putting the bed between us, and one of my windows behind me.

Garrett smiled at that. He was proud of his paranoid creation. It brought to mind what he said about my scars. Priest and Devin were appalled by my marred skin, but Garrett was proud of it. He thought of them like a veteran would battle wounds: hard-earned badges of courage.

He moved toward me, but when I tensed he stopped. "I want to chat, not fight. Will you sit down and relax? You're making me anxious." He nodded to my bed and I looked at it like it too was the enemy. It wasn't of course. I was. My body and my mind had completely different opinions about what a relationship was. Naturally, my body was not nearly as discriminating. "Would you rather we have this conversation with witnesses?" he asked.

"Depends what you're going to say."

"I'm going to say you were right."

"In that case, yes." I perked my brow. He offered me a tight smile, but he wasn't amused by the comment.

"I've been thinking about what you said and I agree. You and me... it's probably not a good idea for us to be fraternizing when you're working toward such an important objective." My stomach lurched. Was that what I said? "I don't think it will work."

I relaxed my defenses. The attack being leveled was no match for my strength or agility. I had submitted the suggestion that we stop seeing each other, but somehow it hurt worse to hear him agree to it. Breaking up was hard to do, even if the relationship wasn't really a relationship.

"Is that okay with you?" he asked.

I shrugged. "I'm not going to beg, if that's what you mean." I crossed my arms, wishing I had left my bra on for this conversation.

He cleared his throat. "I didn't imagine you would mind too much either way. I just hate doing it now. Haden is going to think it was because of what she said. Maybe it is, I don't know." He looked down at the floor and I joined him in the wandering gaze. One never focuses much on a floor except to step on it, until you're reticent with emotion; then it's all you can focus on. "You have all the skills now. You've shown that, when the time comes, you'll use them instead of running away. One more set of bruises and scars isn't going to motivate you more. In fact I think it might have the opposite effect."

I shook my head and hauled my eyes away from the floor. "Wait, what are you saying?"

His brow dipped with annoyance. "I'm saying you and Haden were right." He rolled his eyes at having to say it again. If he could have tasted the words, he might have gagged on them.

"Garrett, are you saying you aren't going to train me?"

"No—yes, but I don't want you to get too relaxed. I don't care what Haden says. August felt the tournaments were where we needed to be, so that is the assumption we should work under. That's why I've been at every competition. She wanted eyes on what's been going on there."

"Yeah, I get that," I said, only slightly interested in the blueprint of our save-the-day plans. "What are you going to have me do then?" I moved and kneeled on the bed. I hadn't intended it to sound dirty, but the sparkle in his eye told me he was thinking otherwise. "For my training," I added.

"I'll leave that to Devin and Haden to figure out. I'll defer to their instincts. At this point it might be best if the three of you regain the camaraderie Haden was referring to. I think Devin's feeling a little underutilized since I've been here."

"So, you're leaving then?" I slumped down and twirled my finger on my quilt. It technically wasn't mine. It was Nicole's, whoever the hell she was. She was another unfamiliar face in a sea of saved souls. She hadn't died in our house, thankfully, or I might not have been able to stay in her room. By the looks of the remaining décor, she couldn't have been more than ten: before rock and roll posters, but after the need for nightlights and teddy bears.

"Do you want me to leave?" He looked surprised by my question, hurt even. I couldn't help but answer truthfully even if it did put me in range of a heart stomping.

"I didn't want you to leave the first time. I don't want you to leave now."

"I—"

"Please don't recite your Chicago obligations speech. I've heard it. I get it. I don't want to hear it ever again. Consider it memorized."

He smirked and moved over to the bed and sat across from me. "Tell me why you put those ugly pajamas on." He nodded to my outfit.

I shrugged. "I didn't figure you were spending the night with me, so there wasn't much point."

"Do you want me to spend the night?" he asked, tracing his finger over the pajama print on my leg.

"Stop asking me what I want. Tell me what you want."

"I want you to not kick me out. I want you to remove these ridiculous little—are these cats or dogs?" He leaned in closer to analyze the fabric.

"Monkeys," I mumbled defensively. "They're cute."

"If you say so. I'd like to just be with you for a change, Lenore. I'd like to focus on this. I know you know my moratorium on a happily ever after with me, so I won't remind you, but if you can't handle that, then you should kick me out now."

"Are you asking me not to fall in love with you?" I narrowed my eyes on him.

He shrugged. "Love comes in many levels. Just don't fall so deep that you can't climb back up."

"You could keep being an asshole. That would ensure I don't." I glared and crossed my arms.

He nodded. "That's true, but I don't want to." He leaned over and kissed my neck. "I want to focus all my energies on evening training."

He tipped my chin back with his cheek and kissed my throat. The action would have translated to an attack in the animal kingdom, but his lips sent shivers into my groin.

"I've never had any objection to those exercises, but what about the morning after?"

"What about the morning after?" He kissed the other side of my neck. I pulled back slightly to look at him.

"Don't take this as an insult to your lovemaking, which is skillful and gratifying, but if I only wanted a good lay, I would be sleeping with Devin." His brow dipped in offense despite my prelude. "I want you to be like this…" I motioned to encompass his body as a whole, "…out there."

"I'll do you anywhere you want." He smirked.

"No, you know what I mean. Be nice out there, so everyone doesn't think I'm a masochist for being with you."

"I'm not very good at nice."

"No, nice doesn't fit you very well, but if you want this…" I motioned to myself this time, "…you're going to have to put it on and break it in until it does fit."

"Do I have to be nice to everyone, or just you?"

I chuckled. "Start with me and fan your way out."

"I'll try." Without warning he pushed me back on the bed, pinning me firmly beneath him. I squealed despite my disgust with squealing in general. "Now, I think we've got too many monkeys jumping on this bed. Let's do something about that."

I couldn't help but laugh as he ripped my pajama bottoms off in disgust. It wasn't how I expected the night to end, but I was happy to know I wasn't going to be covered in bruises for the next few months.

Flying Monkey Business

I SLAMMED INTO THE ground before I even felt his grip on my legs. The wind was knocked out of me from the still frozen albeit snow-free ground. My head hit hard, but my hands were still tangled in his, so I couldn't cradle my forming headache. I wheezed, trying to gather up my air.

With his legs tightly entwined in mine, Devin panted on top of me. "You okay, baby?" I nodded even though I was in a great deal of pain.

"Nice twist, Devin." Garrett applauded from the sidelines. "I guess you did earn your tournament win."

"Who said I didn't?" Devin glared first at him, then at Haden who was sharpening broomsticks for the spear-throwing practice we kept putting off because no one thought it was a relevant fighting skill. She shrugged, not offering any apology for her criticism.

Devin looked back at me and relaxed his hold on my legs and my arms. The change in position left him simply lying on top of me. I knew—whether or not he did—that it was just a display to make Haden jealous. Some things never changed.

I wondered if it would make Garrett jealous, but when I looked back at him, he was testing out Haden's spear. The only one watching us was Priest, but he had been eyeing me all day. He had waited nearly a week for me to probe him about my experience, and apparently he was done waiting.

"You really okay?" Devin asked, brushing my hair from my face. "I thought you were ready for that."

"I fought the best and I lasted a minute. That's pretty good, I think." I smiled, but he didn't smile back. "What's wrong?"

"I just have a lot on my mind right now, and I don't know who to talk to about it. I always used to talk to August, but..." He didn't bother finishing.

"Do you want to talk to me?"

He shook his head. "No matter how I say it, it's going to sound demeaning, but I don't want you to replace her. I know August thought highly of you, but I kind of liked our dynamic before all this happened."

"You want me to continue being a sidekick?" I asked, using my metaphor for our group.

"See, that sounds demeaning. I don't mean it to be, but... I just..."

"You want to be my hero, not the other way around?"

"Yeah," he said with a nod. "That sounds like machismo overload, doesn't it?"

"No, it sounds gallant and servile to a fault. The only objection I have is to your verb tense." He raised an eyebrow. "You already are my hero, Devin." He scoffed at that. "I'm serious. You are the most respectful, attentive, and heroic man I have ever known. I need to change my metaphor, because you are like the tin man in The Wizard of Oz. You're searching for something you already have. August saw how much heart you have, that's why she wanted you by her side. A man with heart is worth dying for."

I could see the pain register on his face, and it took him a moment to contain his grief before he spoke again. "How did you get to be so insightful?"

"Eh, I'm the scarecrow. Straw for brains, but I do manage to get a nugget of truth out once in a while." I chuckled and he joined in.

When the humor faded, he shook his head and lost his smile all together. "No, you're not the scarecrow. You're the cowardly lion. You keep searching for the courage, but it's already there. It comes out when you're defending your friends. That's why August chose you. She knew she was going to die. I think in the back of her mind, she hoped there was a chance you would save her, but that wasn't why she pushed you. She knew when the time came, *your* heart," he tapped my chest, "your lion's heart would fight to the very end to save us. She wanted to make sure you put up a good, *long* fight."

My eyes stung a little and I could see he was working to push back the same emotions. I cleared my throat and as if on cue he rolled off me and we both got up to relieve our teetering breakdowns. "I love you," I said with a strained voice as I walked away.

"I love you too," he said with the same strained voice.

Crackers

T AKING A BREAK FROM the activity outside, I headed in the side door to grab a snack. I had completely forgotten Priest was stalking me until I popped up from the fridge and found him hovering like a hungry vulture. Instead of avoiding him as I had been, I pretended to have no idea what he wanted.

"Summer sausage?" I shoved the tube of processed meat into his face.

He looked it over and nodded. "Please." It wasn't the reaction I was expecting, but he was probably hungry from all his stalker duties: following, observing, observing some more.

I pulled out a jar of cheese and grabbed a box of crackers. Priest reached around me for the knife and cutting board. I grabbed a butter knife from the drawer and we sat at the table to eat our snack.

Priest didn't say anything for a few minutes. We pasted our summer sausage to our crackers with processed cheese spread and satiated our initial hunger. I wiped the cracker crumbs from my shirt and Priest smiled at me.

"Do you need a bib?" he asked.

"It doesn't work. The mere act of putting on a bib guarantees you'll spill into your lap. Murphy's Law, I guess." I reached for the knife just as Priest was going for it. We paused, each trying to offer lead to the other, but in the end I sat back while he cut several more slices off the sausage. "How long do you suppose it will take to run out of food?" I asked, keeping the subject matter blasé. "I mean, before the hunting and gathering has to start back up?"

"I'm sure a lot of people are already doing that." He bit into his sausage without a cracker or cheese. "I guess that's the benefit of being in the boonies—less competition."

"More grim, though. Too many Bible-thumpers in the Midwest." I grimaced as I finished the sentence. "Sorry, I don't mean to—"

"What?" He tipped his brow. "Insult me? Stereotype an entire genre of people?"

"No, piss you off," I groused. "But apparently it comes naturally to me."

"I'm not pissed off, Lenore. I'm amused you keep trying to tiptoe around me, though. I'm not wearing the collar anymore and even if I was, I am a human being just like you. I may have thought I was superior at one time, but clearly..." He sat back, opening his arms in surrender. "I've broken more of the seven deadly sins than anyone here. Let's see, first there was envy." He counted them off on his fingers.

"I was envious of the ones who moved on. Then I was wrathful that I was left behind. Then of course there was lust of women and gluttony of alcohol and drugs. I think sloth also applies to my manner of useless cloistered anti-servitude. And, of course, we can't forget pride. You helped point that one out. So what's left?"

"Greed," I prompted, even though he was probably asking rhetorically. "You haven't been greedy."

"Do you know what the technical definition of greed is?" I shrugged. "An excessive desire to acquire or possess more than what one needs or *deserves*. No, Lenore, I don't think I escaped that particular sin either. Greed is only a stone's throw away from gluttony. Everything I've done since the apocalypse has been for my own satisfaction; pleasurable or self-defeating, it was still for me. So please, don't tiptoe around me like I'm someone of consequence, because I'm not."

Instinctively I reached across the table and touched his hand. Once I had it in my grip, I didn't know what to do with it. I started to draw back, but he leaned forward, following my hand. He took it back into his and rubbed his thumb along the back. It felt good and right. It wasn't sensual. It was just honest human contact.

"Lenore, are you ready to talk to me?"

I glanced around the kitchen as if we were about to start discussing our plot to murder someone. "I don't know, but I kind of get the impression you are. You've been watching me all day like a hawk, and a determined one at that."

"I was enjoying the show, but yes, I would very much like to ask you what you felt when I... Did I hurt you?"

"No." I knitted my brow. "Why are you asking me? Don't you know what you did to me?"

"I don't understand this any more than you understand your gift. I'm running on instinct. You can see the evil in people, whereas I have a grip on this tiny little thread—a connection to... something good." He glanced up rather than bringing up names or labels. "I wanted very much to intensify that connection. Since I feel it strongest when I'm around you, I selfishly decided to use you as a lightning rod. So to speak."

"Did it work?" I asked, squeezing his hand.

"No. For a moment, I felt the connection expand, but as soon as it was done, I was back to a thread again. I'm sorry if I scared you. I took advantage of your aversion to *pissing me off* and talked you into doing something I knew you would be uncomfortable with."

"It scared me, but it wasn't scary. I mean, it was emotionally intense, but it was all my emotion. It wasn't foreign or threatening. It was simply a mirror to my heart history."

Priest nodded.

"I don't mean to shy away from all this. I know it's still important to you even if you don't represent it anymore. I just never got into the pharisaic methods most Christians utilize. Catholicism is about as methodical as you can get without being diagnosed with OCD." Priest chuckled. "Obviously I'm not one to talk since I'm still here, but I never saw God as a being to be worshiped through empty repetitious ceremonies and face-value commitment."

"What did you see Him as?"

I paused, thinking of how to explain what I thought. "As a core, inside of me; inside of everyone." I knew from previous experience any devoted Christian would bristle at the thought of an internalized God. "I'm not saying I'm God. I just mean that my soul... I think it belongs to Him, like..." I took a deep breath, not wanting to go on. Priest was quiet and continued stroking my hand. I appreciated the support, but I hated having this conversation with him of all people. But then again, who else was there?

"I feel like the human soul is connected to that thread you just talked about. In my version, we all have a thread. We don't feel it all the time, but sometimes, in light of dire circumstances or loving circumstances, it can pull at us like we're tethered to Him." I pulled my hand away from Priest. I could barely look at him.

"That's what I think. I don't have a book to tell me so. I don't have a ceremony to acknowledge it. I just think it, feel it, and believe it because it feels right and..." I couldn't believe my eyes were welling with tears. "I don't care if it sounds stupid to you—or to Him, for that matter." I threw my finger up at the proverbial heavens and walked out on him before he could judge me or try to cast his critique on my belief.

What Feels Right

AVOIDING THE MELEE OF spear-throwing—which must have become an effort in futility judging by the laughter resonating from the front yard—I headed behind the garage to hide out from reality for a while. Behind the building was a cluster of trees and overgrowth that would never be thick enough to call a forest. The winter had robbed the trees of leaves, but the ever-present nuisance of cedar trees still offered coverage.

I found a log behind a set of the ugly evergreens and sat down to shake off whatever it was that made talking to Priest so difficult for me. Sometimes we were alike and the humor between us was infectious. Other times it was like he was from a different world, a world I could never and would never be a part of.

Priest said he loved me, but I was still questioning what he meant by that. Like Garrett said, there were many levels to love. Did Priest mean he loved me as he loved all God's creatures? Did he love me because I brought him closer to his one true love? Did he love me like family? Or was his love fueled by human desire?

"You've got to stop running away from me, Lenore." Priest had managed to sneak up on me. That wasn't good. "I know I've pushed you away a good number of times, but that doesn't mean you need to flee my presence when you get uncomfortable or when you think I am."

He rounded my secluded cedars, which clearly hadn't done much to hide me, and sat down beside me on my log. He didn't say anything and neither did I. For a long time, we both sat and stared out at the scenery of cottonwoods and scant remnants of snow. It wasn't much, but it was all there was, and beggars can't be choosers.

At once we both spoke. "What do you want?" we said in unison before blinking and smiling at our mirrored thought process.

"You go. It's your turn to speak," I said.

He grimaced. "I've been raised and trained to do things a certain way. I never questioned it because that was the defined path to God. Now it seems... how did you put it? Pharisaic. I've felt what a true spiritual experience is and I think I'm as addicted to that as I ever was to the drugs and sex. What do you want me to do about that?"

"About your last addiction?"

"Yes. Should I go cold turkey on that as well?"

"Why are you asking me?"

Priest looked around the trees for something before answering. "I don't know if you've noticed this, but you are the only other human being on this Earth who gives a damn about me. I'm asking you because you're my friend, and so far your assessments of me have been pretty dead on. So, does a priest who has divorced God get to seek out spiritual booty calls—okay, that metaphor went too far."

We smiled, but it didn't stay very long. "Priest—"

"I know you know how to say my name. You said it once, you can say it again."

"Don't ask me not to challenge your resolve, and then ask me to call you by your given name. They are mutually exclusive for me."

His eyes widened as he absorbed my full meaning. "Okay," he said simply. "What were you going to say?"

"I don't think you should give up God. I think you should give up trying to please Him. Sometimes trying to do the right thing is different than doing what feels right. I prefer to do what feels right."

"And what feels right, Lenore?"

"Running away always feels right."

"I thought fighting was your new mantra." He smirked.

"No, my mantra is to prepare for the worst, and hope for an escape route." He laughed at me and did a quick silent blessing that he didn't attempt to explain or apologize for. It must have felt right to him.

Collar

"**Y**OU'VE GOT TO BE freaking kidding me!" I yelled up from the backseat of Priest's SUV. The argument had already fizzled out for everyone else, but I was still in the throes of shocked rage and had no intention of letting it go. "You're going to get us killed, Priest!"

"I will not," he said calmly from the driver's seat. He had insisted on driving since it was his vehicle, or at least his acquired property, as most things were for us. Devin had put up a marginal fight for driving his truck, but since it was still dipping below freezing at night, no one was volunteering to ride in the bed of the truck for an hour.

"What are you basing that on? That collar is a representation of a shitload of misery for most of us! You won't be respected, you'll be ridiculed! Take it off!" I wasn't sure what pissed me off more: the fact that he had gone through my drawers to retrieve the collar, that he was intending to wear it to the tournament despite our arguments against it, or that he was being so damned calm about the whole thing.

"Make me," he said, just as calm and quiet as everything else.

I was over the middle seat, breaking apart Devin and Haden, in record time. If Devin hadn't grabbed my legs, I would have reached

Priest's neck before he could defend himself. I wasn't sure if I intended to rip the collar off, or rip his head off.

"Okay," Devin was snickering as he muffled the bulk of his laughter. "Lenore, Lenore, stop. The man is going to wreck if you don't leave him alone." He pulled back on me, but I struggled against him, growling in frustration. Devin could barely hold me because he was laughing so hard. "Garrett, fuck, pull her back. She's going to kill him."

I felt a strong grasp on the waist of my jeans and I was dragged back to my seat. Garrett didn't make any attempts to verbally convince me to stay, but he strapped me into my seat belt rather tightly.

"Devin!" I raged at him as if he wasn't understanding my irritation.

"What do want me to do?" Devin asked, still grinning.

"He's going to get himself killed, and get us hurt in the process."

"That argument has been made, Lenore," Haden snarled. I glared at her, but she just shrugged it off.

"Haden's right." I opened my mouth to protest, but Devin put up a finger to silence me. "We've made our point. There is no reason to continue battering him with words." He glanced at Garrett and I looked over to him for the first time. There was nothing in his expression alluding to a conspiracy, but he shook his head at me and took my hand in his.

It was still strange to have him act so intimately in front of everyone else. I was enjoying the attention, but it still felt foreign, even to me. For a while Haden and Devin tensed at the anomaly of our morning kisses and hand holding as we walked together, but eventually their inclination to protect me subsided.

When I looked back at Devin he nodded to Garrett. I crinkled my brow at this intrigue, but opted to let my anger die back to an ember for the time being. "Fine," I grumbled.

"Pick your battles, lion heart," Devin said before turning around.

I caught Priest looking at me in the rear view mirror. I held his gaze, and, minus glances to the headlight-lit road, he held mine. "Why did you decide to put it back on?" I asked calmly so I didn't irritate everyone.

"I'm not sure," he said. "It felt right."

"You don't have to listen to everything I say," I muttered. I saw Priest smile in the mirror. I broke the eye contact and turned to Garrett. I assumed he would be ignoring me as usual, but this time he was watching me.

I was about to question what was wrong when he kissed me. He gripped my face and pushed his tongue into my mouth. I stifled my desire to groan with pleasure. The longer the kiss went, the more I realized this was not for my benefit. For whatever reason, Garrett felt the need to pee on my leg in front of Priest.

When he finally released me, I gave him a smile to let him know I enjoyed the kiss, but I sat back to discourage any further public displays. With my head down I dared a glance at Priest. He was watching the road, but did eventually glance at me. I immediately felt guilty, like I had flaunted a cookie in front of a starving man. He wasn't starving, though. He wasn't celibate. He could be with a woman anytime he wanted, just not me, apparently. At any rate, I was with Garrett... for now.

Post-apocalyptic relationships were complicated.

Leash

O NCE WE ARRIVED AT the tournament, Priest parked us as close as he could while still maintaining the basic function of the yellow lines. I wanted to object to him entering the building in his collar again, but he was out of the vehicle first and I was the last in line to get out of the side door.

What Priest didn't seem to understand was that in this venue there was bound to be someone with a beef against our *One and Only.* A priest walking into a den of atheists was a bad idea all around. However, in a den of gun-toting, knife-throwing martial artists who haven't ruled out Satanism as a hobby, he was going to be a lamb to the slaughter. Yeah, this was not going to be pretty.

Devin hollered as he jumped out of the vehicle. Haden slid over, but waited for Garrett to get out ahead of her, which was odd since he was in the back seat with me. She followed directly behind him and I heard the scuffle more than saw it, since I was bent over, out of window view.

When I got out, I saw Haden approaching Priest. He was on his knees, struggling between the meaty grips of Devin and Garrett. He looked livid, but he wasn't yelling or cussing them out.

Haden ripped the white collar from his black shirt. Without sympathy for the pained looked on his face, she burned it up with a lighter she pulled from her back pocket. He still didn't speak, but I could see his eyes glaze as he watched the last vestige of his priesthood go up in flames just like his church had four months ago.

Haden leaned over, showing him the melted plastic core. "Did you seriously think we would allow you to endanger us?" Priest looked infuriated, but he shook his head. "Do you remember our conversation on the porch?" He nodded at her. He seemed to understand how to handle Haden. Not many men did. Even Devin forgot sometimes how much of his ego to put aside when dealing with her. "You were on the bottom of the totem, sweetie. Now you're the part that's buried in the ground. I won't lower you again. I'll just put you in the ground, period."

Priest looked her over trying to see if she was serious, but he must have determined she was at least serious enough to consider it, so he nodded again. Garrett and Devin let him go, pushing him to his hands before her. She touched his black button-up shirt. "Change out of this too."

She didn't wait for his response. She walked off, joining Devin and Garrett at the edge of the parking lot. Garrett waved me over and I nodded at him. As I closed the door to the SUV, Priest stalked over and opened the hatch to change his shirt. He was out of my line of sight, but his movements were brisk and forceful so I knew he was fuming. I couldn't help but feel bad. I would never have burned his collar. I knew how important it was to him, even if it was just a security blanket.

I tiptoed around the back as he pulled out a tight long-sleeved t-shirt and started unbuttoning his shirt. "You should have taken it off when I asked," I mumbled.

He ripped his shirt off, pausing to glare at me. I didn't want to look him in the eyes, but I also didn't want my eyes to roam his bare chest. "You didn't ask me to take it off! You just battered me with your derision!" He slipped the gray t-shirt over his head. I noticed he was still wearing my necklace. That brought me some comfort, but I wasn't sure why.

"Would you have taken it off if I had—?"

"Yes!" he snapped.

"I don't believe you."

"Then don't." He slammed the hatch shut, not taking into consideration my proximity. I jumped back, and he paused to look me over before he continued. "I felt like I had to put it on. Like I needed to show... I didn't mean to endanger the group. I could have stayed separate from you."

"I was worried about you, you stubborn ass."

"I'm sorry, did you just call *me* a stubborn ass? First of all, that's redundant, and you are way more stubborn than me."

"No it's not. Stubborn mule would be redundant, and yes, I know. That's why I'm standing here happily enduring your wrath sans collar."

"Happily enduring my wrath? This is you happy?" he asked, crossing his arms.

"A little guilty, but yeah. I'm happy you aren't going to get killed tonight."

"You didn't know that." He started walking, but I grabbed his arm.

"Don't," I said firmly. "Don't underestimate everyone else's pain just because you think you've found your way again. These people... Everyone is pretending to have fun at a party, when they really just want to go home. You can't walk in and remind them they don't have a ride. We all get it now, Priest. We all believe. We all know and it fucking sucks. Ignorance really is bliss.

"That collar was not your connection or your livelihood. That collar was your last bit of pride. The part of you that thought you were above us all, or that you needed to save us. You aren't and you don't. I'm sorry she burned it, but I'm glad it's gone. If it makes you feel any better, maybe you felt it was right to wear it because you needed to have that lesson refreshed."

Priest's eyes widened as he considered the prospect of an unwitting penance. He relaxed and nodded to me. He might not have agreed, but he couldn't dismiss the possibility.

I headed toward Garrett and the others. As I suspected, Garrett was watching our conversation with interest. I took a few jogging steps to reach him faster, and he smiled before wrapping his arm around me. I was starting to like this public affection.

Tell Me I Didn't Just Say That

Once again, the tournament had changed its patina. The champagne-popping red carpet party of the previous month had transformed into a cross between a rock concert and a demo derby. We were informed at the doors that the box seats were still reserved for us and we headed there.

We were still photographed and battered with questions, but the questions this time were all about August. One reporter seemed to have figured out that Garrett was her half-brother and tried to extrude information about their childhood. Consciously or unconsciously Garrett squeezed my hand at the mention of it. I squeezed back, and he relaxed under the reporter's scrutiny.

With far fewer questions answered than asked we maneuvered into the stadium. I let go of Garrett's hand to get through the door. I could see over Devin's head the full extent of the tournament's facelift. The music blared louder than any eardrums could reasonably tolerate. Random piles of dirt were added to the sand in the main arena. In the center were a group of women dressed like cheerleaders performing dramatic AACCA banned stunts.

The crowd gasped at each catapulted girl, and cheered for her safe return. There was a mix of mismatched styles in the crowd, as usual, but overall this was a Sunday-best event for most people.

"Ladies?" Devin protruded his elbows to me and Haden. Instinctively I latched on and let him lead me away. A few steps down I thought to look back at Garrett to see if I was offending him, but he was hanging back with Priest, having what looked like an in-depth conversation. Even though neither of them looked angry—or perhaps *because* they didn't—I didn't like it.

Halfway down the stairs, Devin froze in his tracks. I followed his glaring eyes to the cause of his trepidation. Adrian Dorn was in the mayor's box, cheering on the performance with the rest of the crowd. From this distance, he was still a beautiful man with an endearing smile— one that had drawn me in from across the stadium the first time I felt it aimed at me.

"We aren't here to fight him," I reminded Devin and Haden though I might as well have been invisible. I looked back at Priest and Garrett for help, but their intense conversation had halted as they glared at Adrian as well.

I wanted to avenge my friend's death, but every instinct I had about Dorn told me he was more dangerous than he seemed. If that was true, then I didn't want him on our bad side. Not until we were ready, anyway.

I pulled away from Devin and skipped a few steps as I made my way down to our box before veering over to the mayor's box. Adrian caught my eye on the way and his face melted into sympathy. It seemed so honest and heartfelt, it was easy to be deceived by him.

"Lenore," he said too quiet to hear over the music, but I could read his lips. He stepped out of his box and met me above the entryway like last time. "I'm so sorry," he said louder.

He put his hand on the rail as if he wanted to touch my shoulder in condolence, but was too shy to actually do it. Very easy to be deceived. I put my hand up as well, not far from his. In a way, I knew he was drawing me in, but I was also drawing him in. Part of me wished I was mistaken about his demeanor, but I knew I wasn't.

He reached to touch my hand, but the mayor sidled up between us and interrupted him. His balding head shined from the bright lights above us. "Ms. Evans, I am so sorry about the incident last month. Your friend was a valiant fighter and I have no doubt she will be remembered by the entire country."

"Thank you." I glanced at Adrian. He looked annoyed by the disruption, but kept a tight smile on his face like any good employee would.

"Adrian here has personally seen to it that it will never happen again." Mayor Thompson put a tight arm around Adrian. "Haven't you?" he asked with menace through his grand toothy smile.

"Yes," Adrian agreed. "We've placed spotters in the stands to watch each competitor and we are implementing a secondary search prior to releasing the grim into the arena to check for shivs." He directed the amendments to me, but I knew they were for the mayor's sake.

"Good, good." Mayor Thompson gave him a firm squeeze before trading his attention to another man passing. He was gone without a goodbye.

"Sorry." Adrian looked embarrassed. "He's kind of..." He glanced behind him to make sure he was gone. "A douche."

I laughed. "Yeah, well, politics hasn't changed much. None of this has, really." I scanned the crowd that was enjoying the Cirque Du Soleil of cheerleading acts.

"How so?" Adrian asked, drawing my attention back to him. His eyes locked onto mine and for a moment I forgot what I was saying.

"Um... more. We all still want more. The money is useless, but we still want power," I nodded back to reference the mayor, "or fame," I looked to the arena floor. "It's always something."

"More can be better, if it's more of the right thing." Adrian wet his lips.

At some point his fingers had become entangled in mine on the railing, but I wasn't sure when. I expected to feel the strange repulsion I usually felt, but instead I felt drawn to him. I couldn't understand what had changed. He leaned forward and I knew he wanted to kiss me, but I couldn't move. I couldn't for even a moment think of the reason I hated this man.

"You must be Adrian Dorn." Priest's voice could have been a thousand miles away or inches, I wasn't sure yet. Adrian's eyes narrowed and shifted to look over my shoulder. "I've heard a lot about you," Priest said.

Adrian glared at him, but his eyes widened in shock for a moment before returning to his narrowed gaze. I was finally able to look away from Dorn. Priest was not far behind me. I expected him to be glaring as well, but he was impassive. Behind him another few steps, I saw Garrett. He seemed to be playing backup to Priest.

I didn't understand why Adrian was so irritated, but then I noticed my cross necklace hanging openly against Priest's shirt. I could feel a tingling in my spine as the creepy-crawly feeling returned. I wanted to let go, but I forced myself to see what my strange talent would uncover.

Cold swept through my body and unintelligible images started to flash through my mind like a slide show. The conversation between Priest and Dorn went on, but I faded into my own thoughts.

I could feel arousal and pain, neither more powerful than the other. I could taste iron and salt in my mouth. My stomach roiled and I resisted the urge to gag. The imagery became clearer and I could see Adrian on top of me, and inside me.

We were both completely naked and covered in blood. I could feel him moving against me. It was ecstasy and anguish with each movement. It felt real. It felt good, and it felt so wrong. I could smell something burning. All at once I realized the blood smearing his body was mine.

I ripped my hand from Adrian's and leaned over the railing holding my head. I could sense the fluster behind me and I immediately made my excuses. "Oh, this music is giving me a headache."

"Are you alright, Lenore?" Dorn touched my hand, and someone touched my back. I whirled around and found Garrett directly behind me. Priest hadn't moved, but he was watching me carefully, trying to discern what was happening.

"I'm so sorry, migraine." I touched my forehead and chuckled. "We can hardly have a conversation, Mr. Dorn." I shrugged and the suspicion on his face was alleviated.

"Can I get you something?" He was caressing my hand. The imagery was gone, but his touch still felt wrong and inhuman. Between my claustrophobic affliction and his creep factor, I was about ready to jump out of my skin, but I remained cool.

"I need some air." I glanced at Garrett and he shifted to let me by. "Thank you." I squeezed Adrian's hand and moved away as quickly as I could without being obvious about my revulsion.

Priest let me by as I walked past our box seats to find an exit. Haden and Devin were watching, waiting for an explanation. Devin started to stand, but I gave him a slight head shake and he immediately sat back down. I could feel Garrett following me, but he stayed back as if he was in no hurry to catch up with me. He didn't want to make my display more obvious; he was a smart man.

I'm Okay, I'm Okay

B Y THE TIME I got to an exit, I was already shaking and gagging from my memories, or premonitions, or whatever I had just witnessed. The taste of iron and salt in my mouth was only imaginary, but the thought of my own blood, and his...

I vomited behind a sculpture in the front of the building. I intended to make it to the sax player, but I only made it to the mime. Garrett came up behind me to console me or pump me for information, perhaps both. He touched my back and I recoiled.

"Don't touch me right now, okay?" I backed away to the center cluster of sculptures that were basically gigantic blocks and balls. A few new artistic touches had been added—via graffiti, but there was room for improvement anyway.

"What's wrong with you? What did you feel from him? What's his plan?"

"No plan, just a sick fantasy," I said, leaning against the base of what I could only assume was a gigantic electric fan sculpture. "At least I hope that's not his plan."

"What did you see?" Garrett came closer and I put up a hand to stop him.

"Please don't ask me. I just need a minute to wash my brain out." I slid down the concrete slab and Garrett seemed to debate with himself what to do.

"I don't want to leave you here."

"Just wait inside the doors. I'll only be a few minutes. Ten tops."

"Are you sure you're okay?"

"No, Garrett, I'm not. That's why I need ten minutes." I gave him a pained smile and he seemed to understand. He hesitated another moment as if he thought he should still persist to stay with me in spite of my objection. I couldn't blame him—women rarely verbalized what they really wanted, but at that moment I didn't want any man with carnal knowledge of me anywhere near me.

I sat for the first minute after he left with my eyes closed, listening to the various voices of the people outside and the distant thump of the music inside. The images from Dorn were on instant replay in my mind and no matter what I did I couldn't erase them. They were erotic and disturbing, made scarier by the fact that I knew how easily he had drawn me into him.

If Priest hadn't interrupted...

If his necklace hadn't set him off...

"Priest?" I whispered half hoping and half knowing he would be there.

"Yes." His voice answered from behind the sculpture some-where.

I sniffled back some tears at hearing him there. "I don't want to do this anymore."

"Do what, Lenore?" He was to my left, but he still hadn't come over to me.

"I don't want to be some freaky mind reader. I don't want to be a superhero." He stepped around one of the ball sculptures and gave me a sympathetic look. He started to open his mouth to speak, but I interrupted him. "Don't tell me about courage, and chosen paths, and strength of character or I'll claw your eyes out."

"Okay," he said simply and crouched down by his sculpture not coming any closer. "I can help you, if you'll let me. I can ease your pain."

I shook my head. "I don't want anyone else in my head tonight. I don't want anyone... anywhere..." I clenched my teeth and hit my head against the block behind me. I wanted this conflicting feeling out of my mind.

"Just grab my hand, Lenore," Priest whispered and I shook my head. "Let me do this for you. I have so little to offer you."

I looked over to him, and I could see his calm passive façade was chipping away. He was torn between doing as I asked, and doing what was right. Just like Garrett, he was stuck in the gray area of when to push and when not to push a woman. He was also worried. He couldn't comfort me the way he wanted to for a good number of reasons. He couldn't talk to me the way he wanted to because I was rarely comforted by religious rhetoric or clichéd encouragements. All he could do was ask, and hope I would say yes.

I reached out my hand and closed my eyes. He moved forward and gripped my hand. I didn't mean to rip it away, but it was done before I realize I was doing it. "I'm sorry," I mumbled into my knees as I clasped my hands over my head.

Priest started to murmur something in Latin and I could feel him getting closer to me. When he was close enough, he rested his hand very gently on my head, and I didn't flinch. The warmth that spread over me was contradictory to what I felt with Adrian. Priest was a good man and there was no denying that, even if he didn't agree.

I fought back the tears like I could simply hold my breath and will them away, but the pull to release was too strong. Priest touched my hand, but this time I didn't pull away. I gripped his hand back tightly.

I waited for the dizzying emotional rollercoaster, but my pinnacle of tears was followed by something different. An emotional teddy bear settled into me and I could feel the tension inside of me drain like water from a faucet.

I lifted my head to take in a long-needed breath and Priest moved his hands to my face. He was still chanting something, but it sounded like poetry at the moment. I cupped his hands and drank in whatever this offering was. I didn't care where it came from or what it meant. I wanted to bask in it.

I could feel his lips kiss my forehead and he started to draw himself away from me. "No, please," I begged to keep the feeling.

"It's okay," he said in the tiniest of whispers. "It'll linger." I heard him sniffle and I opened my eyes. He looked wrung out and his eyes were red from salty tears.

"Priest." I reached out to him, but this time he pulled away from me.

"It's okay."

"What did you do?" I stood and he followed, taking a step back before I could try to get near him again. "Priest?"

"I just used me. I wasn't sure what He would do to you. I didn't want to overload you again."

I shook my head. As strange as I found my special gift, I still couldn't fathom his. "You took all my pain into you, didn't you?"

"It was a tradeoff. You got the better deal, I'm afraid." He smiled... a little. "I gave you a little box of chocolates, priest-style."

"Oh, Priest." I started to move forward, but quickly remembered he was in no mood for hugs. "You really know how to make a girl feel inadequate." I chuckled, but he seemed even more pained by the statement. "Thank you for that, but please don't do it again. I'm not sure what's worse: feeling that way, or watching you feel it."

"He must have shown you something pretty bad to make you feel this way," Priest said.

I couldn't help but look away. The memory of Adrian wasn't as clear in my mind, but I knew that Priest was feeling what I had felt and it embarrassed me. He probably expected the fear, disgust, and pain, but I'm sure the arousal was not what he had in mind when he started. I opened my mouth to try to defend the feeling like a case of hiccups, but he didn't want an explanation right now.

"You should go back in. Your ten minutes are up," he said. I knew he wanted to be rid of me, but I was stuck with the same decision he and Garrett struggled with: do what he wants or what he needs? I decided that in this not so dissimilar case to my own, solitude was desired and necessary. Priest's emotions—mine—were without reference to the origin, which most likely made the feelings even more uncomfortable with me around.

"Sure," I said, sounding slightly defeated, and headed back into the events center.

Heartache: Double Dose

I REACHED FOR THE framed glass door, but I didn't pull on it. I could see Garrett inside the vestibule, talking to a woman I didn't recognize. He was smiling at her. The strangeness of the expression alone was enough to stop me in my tracks.

I could only see the back of the woman, but I could already tell she was gorgeous. She had coppery red hair with long billowing curls like every woman thinks they want, but would hate to mess with every day. She was in a white dress that could have been casual or dressy depending on the accessories. The stilettos beneath her chiseled calves brought her nearly an inch taller than Garrett.

I tried not to make any assumptions about their relationship when she reached around and hugged him cordially, but that was only the beginning. She leaned back and she kissed him full on the lips. Again, I pleaded with the green streak stabbing my heart that he wasn't backing the kiss. However, when his fingers tangled into her hair and he pulled her closer, I felt that green streak turn red.

So much for lying to myself.

I slipped in the doors beside another couple and headed through the commons to the arena doors. When I looked back Garrett caught sight of me. For a moment, he looked worried, but he quickly turned back to his lady friend with a smile. I never got smiles.

Back in the arena, I settled into the box seat next to Devin and Haden. He drew his arm up around me to match the one he already had for Haden. "Hey, what happened with Dorn?"

"He doesn't seem to have any plans for tonight, at least none that will come true." He perked an eyebrow at me and I leaned into his shoulder. "What's tonight's competition again?"

"It's a hat trick tonight. Outdated weaponry, homemade small-scale explosives... you name it, it will be here tonight."

"This should be interesting," I said.

The newest announcer came into the ring following the exit of the performers. She was naturally sexy and beautiful. Her entrance received the usual catcalls and whistles, one of which was from Devin. She was *almost* wearing a tuxedo, but the cummerbund was being used as a bandeau. She skipped the jacket and only wore the silver vest, and in place of the pants was the white button-up shirt tied like a wrap skirt. However, the wrap didn't fully cover her so her entire right leg was essentially bare. The strangest part about the outfit was that she was pulling it off.

"Lenore," Garrett whispered from the seat behind me. "We need to talk." I glanced back at him, searching the background for his redhead.

"Not now," I said and turned back around. Devin noted the scene, but didn't ask about it.

"Lenore?" Garrett went so far as to touch my shoulder. Devin gripped me a little tighter and looked back at him.

"She said not now," Devin said firmly. There must have been a nonverbal plea of some kind, because Devin sighed, looked me over, and rebutted his request with a little less irritation. "She's watching the show. Let's just enjoy the night."

I could hear Garrett slump back in his chair after he released me. He wasn't happy about me cowering behind Devin, but then again, since I was mad first, I considered his anger irrelevant. Besides that, I wasn't interested in explanations from him.

Garrett had always been honest about his lack of commitment to me, but I thought my disinterest in multiple relationships had been enough to convey my desire for a monogamous relationship. I had considered he might have girlfriends in Chicago, but I never expected to see one of them. Now that I had seen one of them, I didn't know how I felt about it. I didn't know if I could share.

Share and Share Dislike

A s I LOOKED OUT onto the arena I remembered the last time I was in this box. The celebration was different, the competitions were different, but this was still the same location. This was the place where I tried and failed to save my best friend, my bloodless sister, and my hero.

The fireworks encircling the arena spat out sparks not far from us, making me jump. In several areas around the stadium minor fires started, but they were quickly put out by the increased security and safety amendments.

"Ladies and gentlemen, and those of you not falling into those categories," the announcer drawled making the crowd cheer, "we have a special treat for you tonight. As you know, our previous tournaments have been in defensive specialties, but tonight… tonight you get to see all the crap we didn't know what to do with." The crowd roared with laughter and applauded. The energy was palpable and I couldn't help but get involved despite my sour mood.

The first round of competition was a battleground melee lasting almost an hour. They poured grim into the arena and men toppled them with maces, clubs, blow darts—which turned out to be laughably useless on crystallized skin—Trekkie-inspired weaponry, and last but not least, small explosives.

Though impractical for real combat, a gaunt twenty-something geek stole the show with his squib-filled mud balls. The brute tactics of the others were admirable, but Cody Dodd took first place because he was effortlessly blowing up grim long after his competitors had worn out. In the end, the only thing that stopped him was the lack of solution to make his sticky mud balls.

I glanced over to Dorn on occasion and each time I found him watching the competition intently. I didn't look too long though, because he inevitably sensed me watching him and would look over. I wasn't entirely sure what I had felt from him. The attraction between us was magnetic, but there was also something very dark inside him that wanted to harm me.

Since I didn't feel the carnal revulsion until Priest had irritated him, I wondered if Dorn was capable of radiating timid charm to disguise his ulterior motives. August had told me my attraction to him might not be sexual, but instead visceral. If I was able to sense evil in people, it was not far-fetched to presume I would then be drawn to it like a beacon. If that was true, then Dorn was a very strong beacon of evil.

Round two of the competition was more of the same, minus the elimination of the lesser fighters: the dart-blowers and the Trekkies. Klingon bat'leths are—big shock—difficult to wield in a real battle situation. Unfortunately, the lack of comic relief took some of the fun out of the entertainment.

Priest finally returned and sat behind us with a chair between Garrett and him. I looked back to see if he was okay, but he wouldn't hold my gaze. I turned a little further to see Garrett and he took advantage of my attention and leaned closer.

"We need to talk. Please," he added when it was clear I had no intention of doing his bidding. Somehow the simple niceties of please and mother-may-I were all it took to break my stubborn resolve. Perhaps that was something Garrett should have been informed of eight months ago as well.

I nodded somberly and stood up. I signaled to Devin that I was going to step out and he looked between me and the arena. He couldn't readily find the balance between chivalry and entertainment. Garrett stood and placed his arm behind me, ushering me to exit with him. Devin seemed satisfied that he didn't need to go with me and settled back in to watch the show.

As I shuffled past Priest on my way out of the box, I noticed he had removed his necklace. He was gripping it so tightly in his hand I expected to see drops of blood on his pants. My concern for tetanus aside, I was afraid he might have put his mind at risk by helping me.

Garrett pressed gently on my back, keeping me from questioning Priest verbally or otherwise. We shuffled through the fire code prohibited audience and exited the arena. There was a handful of people in the commons area running in and out of the restrooms. Plus a few couples participating in less socially acceptable forms of PDA, but for the most part, we were alone.

I found a random spot against a wall and leaned against it. I was going for casual, but I wasn't sure why. Before I was mad, but now with the anger down to embers, I felt wounded. I didn't necessarily love Garrett, but I did respect him enough not to seek out another man's attentions—certainly not right in front of him.

"I need to explain what you saw," he started.

"No, you don't," I interrupted gently. "You've been very clear with me." I cleared my throat, trying not to let the emotion of the moment get ahead of my words. "I misunderstood your moratorium on our relationship. I thought you couldn't be with me because of the long-distance thing. I didn't realize it was because you wanted to freely fuck other women." I rekindled my anger faster than I could clamp my mouth shut.

"Lenore, it's not what you think," he objected.

"Oh Christ, don't use that tired old line. Look, I get it. This is the post-apocalyptic world. Life sucks, why would anyone want to devote themselves to one person? But I thought while we were together it would be just us. I guess short-term monogamy is still too much to ask of a man these days."

"Lenore, I'm not cheating on you—"

I didn't give him a chance to finish. "You know, at least Devin was always honest about his polygamy."

His face contorted with disgust. "I am nothing like Devin. I have only ever been with three women my entire life: my high school sweetheart, you, and my wife." My mind blanked, as I'm sure my face did. I couldn't quite understand the words despite them being spoken clearly in the language of my birth. "I'm not cheating on you with that woman, Lenore. I'm cheating on her with you."

My foot slipped off the wall, and I was no longer cool and casual. If the wall fell I would have fallen with it. The truth punched me in the gut, which was bad enough, but then it danced around me and laughed at me.

Garrett said he had obligations in Chicago. Never in a million years did I think he meant a wife. So many people post apocalypse were left alone without family. It never occurred to me that someone might still be living out their happily ever after *after* the apocalypse.

Garrett had been reluctant to get close to me at first, like he wanted me to make the first move. He wouldn't even speak to me when August was around. She surely would not have approved of her brother cheating. She definitely wouldn't have approved of me getting hurt by him.

"We've been together ten years," he started when it was clear I was properly caught up.

"Please don't tell me, you were having trouble and then the apocalypse only tore you farther apart, because I saw you kiss her. That wasn't a prelude to a divorce kiss."

"You're right, it wasn't. The truth is we were happily married with three children." I winced at the thought of being a home-wrecker. "Our children moved on, but we didn't."

I looked up at him and saw something I had never seen before: It was the same impassive face that rarely smiled and almost never laughed, but now I knew why. He wasn't just a hard personality to crack. He was a man in mourning. He was filled top to bottom with pain over the loss of his children, anger that he couldn't go with them, and a determination to do right by his sister, posthumously or otherwise.

"I'm so sorry." My eyes prickled with empathetic tears. Even though I had no connection with his children, I understood loss, as we all did.

"We still love each other very much," he admitted. "I can't lie about that." I put on a thin smile that hopefully conveyed my happiness for his love. My bitterness hadn't fully set in yet, and logic was prevailing to keep up a minimum of social criteria. "Being with her all the time would ruin us. August asked for my help and I gladly took on the duty so I could be away from her."

"Why?" I asked, presuming I had missed the step leading to this conclusion.

"Because losing three children simultaneously is not something a marriage can survive. We love each other, but every time..." He paused, looking away from me to collect himself. Whatever anger I had for him melted into a desire to hold him. "Every time I look at her, I see my daughter. And every time she looks at me, she sees our sons." He cleared his throat, trying to filter the emotion from his voice.

"I don't even know what to say. I don't know what to do."

"What do you feel?" he asked. "Not that it won't change a hundred times before sunrise, but what do you feel right now?"

"I want to hold you," I said. There were other feelings trying to push through, but at that moment, all I wanted to do was make him feel as warm as Priest had made me feel earlier.

Garret stepped forward, giving me the only permission I needed to take him in my arms. I couldn't offer the deep teddy bear consolation that Priest could, but I could pocket my fears and misgivings for another day.

Fantasy

T HE MORNING AFTER THE tournament was as close to an inquisition as I've ever experienced. The palpable discomfort between me and Garrett made sure the topic of Dorn didn't come up on the way home, but in the fresh, nearly-noon light, everyone was eager to hear more.

"What did he say? What did you feel?" Devin leaned over the table. Haden was beside me with her foot on my chair. When I didn't answer right away, she gave my thigh a shove with her foot. I glanced at Priest who was still asleep in the living room, having never made it upstairs to August's room. I had checked him more than once to make sure he was still breathing. I presumed using his internal energies to absorb my emotions had drained him. Or he was just very tired.

"We barely spoke. He expressed concern about August," I started.

Garrett scoffed, but didn't turn from his pancake flipping at the stove.

"What did you feel?" Haden asked like I was retarded. "Isn't that what this was all about? What are the inner workings of his plot?"

"I don't know. I didn't get that far."

"You were upset by something," Devin said, unhappy with my less-than-explicit answer. "How far did you get?"

"When I first touched him there was nothing. He seemed fine. I..." I suddenly remembered that it wasn't fine. I had been captivated by him. I was entranced by more than a copulatory gaze. He was doing something to me. If Priest hadn't interrupted, it might have been more than my mind that needed a bath.

Devin touched my hand, bringing me back to the table. Garrett chose that moment to sit a plate of pancakes down right between us, effectively shooing Devin's hand from mine. Given his admission last night I was surprised he was being so territorial. I had yet to address that particular enlightenment, but I was pretty sure it wasn't going to bring Garrett and me closer.

The only reason I didn't kick him out to sleep in August's room was because of the hurt I had witnessed in him. No matter how mad I was about the lies, I couldn't begrudge him a warm body. Though I was tepid to his affections, he persisted to make love to me, and this time it did feel like we were making love.

"I'm not certain about anything," I started again as we all loaded up on pancakes. "I think Dorn has some abilities like me. When I first read him he drew me in, but I didn't feel anything bad. When Priest came over flashing his religious paraphernalia, Dorn got irritated and I started to feel something from him. Feel, taste, smell..."

"What?" Devin asked with a mouth full of food.

I glanced at Haden, hoping for a little support, but she wasn't going to let me get by with *I don't want to talk about it*. Garrett joined us at the table and Priest finally shuffled in groggily, fumbling through the cupboard for a clean coffee cup. Thank goodness, every man in the house was available to hear about Dorn's sadist fantasy with me.

Yay!

I exhaled and tried to explain it delicately. "I saw a vision of Dorn and me... together... carnally."

"What?" Devin's head shot up. If Dorn had been there right then, Devin would have been beating the shit out of him. "If that fucker tries to rape you, I'll rip his fucking dick off." Pancake bits flew out of his mouth as he cussed.

Mortified by his translation, my eyes searched the room. Haden was beginning to glean my discomfort, but she wouldn't be any help to me until she understood for sure. Garrett was as wide-eyed as Devin. Priest glanced at me, but I looked away. He knew first hand that my vision was not exactly a forced event. Although it was painfully sadistic, it was most certainly pleasurable.

"The vision wasn't rape. It was consensual. It was very real and very scary. I don't want to discuss it in detail."

"Wait a minute." Devin dropped his fork. "Was this a premonition? Or is this his future plot?"

"I don't know. I assumed it was his fantasy."

"Should we be worried? Are you attracted to this fucker?" Devin said coldly. I couldn't believe what he was suggesting, and *him* of all people. I would never betray them by sleeping with the enemy.

"No," I whispered a less-than-forceful defense and tapped my fork on my plate.

"Devin, stop, she can't be responsible for what goes on in his mind." Haden was finally there to defend me, but too late.

"You said he drew you in last night. The truth is you haven't been able to stay away from him since you walked into that auditorium. Maybe it's not you he wants. Maybe it's you who wants him. Maybe it wasn't his fantasy you were seeing."

My mouth gaped and I struggled to find a defense to the accusation. I dropped my fork, suddenly without appetite. I expected someone to object when I stood, but everyone was stuck between the shock of Devin's accusation and their curiosity to hear my answer.

There was no point holding anything back now. Propriety aside, I was on trial because no one, including me, understood what my special talent was trying to tell us. Devin was probably still mad I hadn't explained the incident with Priest. Being presented with another exclusion was too much for him to tolerate.

"The vision I had was pleasurable, but it was also painful. We were covered in blood—my blood. I could taste it right along with his semen. I smelled burning flesh, and judging by the pain resonating through my body, I was the one being burned. When I say it was consensual, I only meant I wasn't fighting him off. I didn't mean I wanted it."

Devin's eyes widened and he started to speak, but Priest gripped his shoulder tightly. Before he could slough him off, his body went into convulsions as if he might puke up his breakfast. Garrett and I exchanged confused looks before he barreled over Priest.

Tricks and Triggers

"WHAT THE FUCK DID you do to him?" Haden jumped the table to check Devin, who was wide-eyed and panting like he had seen a ghost.

Garrett was kneeling over Priest, not sure what to do with him now that he had him down. Priest was looking at Devin with as much interest as Haden, like he didn't quite understand what he had done either. I was uselessly standing on the sidelines, waiting for someone to tell me which team I was supposed to be playing for.

"Devin?" Haden smacked his cheek.

"Ouch, don't. I'm fine, get off me." Devin pushed her away and looked to me for an explanation which he must have deemed useless, because he turned around to look at Priest. "What was that?"

Priest glanced at me like he wasn't sure he should answer. "I gave you a taste of what Adrian made her feel last night."

"What?" everyone said, including me.

Priest glanced at me again, still seeking permission. Garrett let him sit up, but stayed on the floor with him in case he planned on *zapping* anyone else. "I wanted you to feel her pain. Your accusations are outrageous. You need to understand what kind of a beast Dorn is. He was manipulating her. It would take someone very vigilant to see through his façade."

"Let's go back to step one." Devin stood, intentionally towering over Priest. "When did you get the ability to… do whatever you just did?"

"I've been developing some skills, much like Lenore, although perhaps a little more varying in usage."

"What, is *everyone* a freaking psychic now?" Haden scoffed, looking at me. I shrugged. "Is that what he did to you the other night when you were screaming?"

"No," Priest answered before I could. I was glad, since I still didn't know what to call that. "Similar, but not for the same purpose. I didn't hurt her. I just surprised her." Devin looked at me for confirmation. I nodded. "I would never hurt her," Priest added.

I could see Devin start to connect the emotions Priest had just given him to the description of my vision. It was dawning on him how inappropriate his accusation was. He looked at Haden a wordless request in his anguished eyes.

"Come on, you two." Haden moved over to Garrett and Priest and practically kicked them to get them on their feet and out of the kitchen. "Let's go house shopping, so I don't kill someone."

Priest and Garrett showed some reluctance in leaving, but given the way Devin had treated me, and the confession it extruded, there was certainly room for some alone time. When they were coated up and out the door, Devin looked down at the floor. Oh, the fascination of the floor; if only the answers were written there.

"I was out of line," Devin finally said daring a glance up at me. I didn't want to agree with him, but I also didn't want to defend his attack.

"I didn't mean to be secretive. It just wasn't something I wanted to share, certainly not over the breakfast table."

"I know. I understand that now, but..." His jaw tensed. "August kept so much to herself. She was so damned quiet about her hopes and fears. As much as I loved her, I hate her for leaving us like this." He motioned to the proverbial this. "We have no idea what we are doing, because she never let us in. I don't want you to start keeping secrets too."

I looked down at the floor, hoping to find my own answers. It didn't illuminate me to anything other than its need to be mopped. "I'm sorry," I said.

Devin stood and reached out his hand to me. I took it and he towed me up and wrapped his arms around me. "I'm so sorry, baby." He took in a stuttered breath and kissed my temple. "I won't let him hurt you, I promise. We're going to figure this out and we're going to make that bastard pay for everything he's done."

I tightened my grip around him. I was confident we would be able to take down Dorn, but I wasn't certain we could do it without someone getting hurt in the process.

Monogamy and Other Such Fairy Tales

"I DON'T WANT A new house," I argued from the back of the SUV, behind Haden and Devin. It had occurred to me the seed for this change had originated from me, but I was regretting it.

"Just look at it," Haden insisted, leaning over the seat. "It has three bathrooms, four bedrooms, a formal dining table seating six, and a double fireplace."

"Why didn't you guys ever get a bigger place before?" Priest asked from the driver's seat. "There must be plenty of mansions going unused."

"Too much space," Haden answered. "Too many places for grim to hide. Besides that, most of the nice houses are in neighborhoods in town, and that's not an option. The grim still inhabiting the surrounding homes could surround us in the night. Assuming they could get coordinated."

"I wouldn't put it past them," Garrett responded beside me. "They may be pretty zombie-like when they first animate, but I've seen some old grim in Chicago that are like vampires: quicker than humans and a hell of a lot smarter. Luckily it doesn't take a wooden stake to kill them. Any stake will do, or a gun, or a hard punch to the head."

Haden, to my surprise, smiled at Garrett's morbid humor. He looked at me to see if his joke had tickled me and I smiled to give him credit for it. He wrapped his arm around me and kissed me deeply.

It was a lot of PDA for him, but he had been steadily getting more aggressive with his affections since he told me he was married. It was as if he realized he could be the one to lose me. Instead of giving me space to decide if I still wanted to be in a relationship with him, he was clutching onto me tighter and tighter. The only reason I wasn't fighting him on it was because I felt bad for his situation. I didn't want to abandon him.

When Garrett let me go I again put on a smile to match his affection. The more he asked of me, the less energy I could muster to reciprocate. I wasn't sure I had ever fallen in love with him, but if I had, I was slowly rising out of it.

He leaned back in his seat and I caught Priest's eye in the rear view mirror. I couldn't tell from his eyes what he was thinking. Was he jealous? Did it matter? Priest was not available. Devin and I were beyond a sexual relationship. Dorn was a sadistic, murderous, evil fuck—so that wasn't going to work out. In the end, Garrett was all I had. I might as well not get too fussy about monogamy and other such fairy tales.

House Hunting

THE HOUSE WAS BEAUTIFUL. It was a log cabin design on the outside, but it was modern on the inside. I could see why Haden suggested we see it. The kitchen, dining room, and living room were open with a step down from the kitchen into the dining room/living room. The long wooden table in the dining room area was big enough to seat six. The front door, and the back door—which exited from the living room to a deck—were the only entrances. Much like the other house they would be easy to guard. No one could sneak in without us seeing.

Beyond the living room was the master bedroom with a master bath. The master bedroom shared the double-sided fireplace with the living room. It was something I had never hoped to have during my real life, because of the expense. Beyond the kitchen was a guest toilet, followed by three bedrooms, all of them relatively the same size, sharing one large bathroom.

"What do you think?" Haden asked after we had viewed it and rejoined in the kitchen around the marble island. "There isn't another house for about a mile. It's next to a main road. We'd be closer to town, but a little farther from the O." She ran through the location details like a professional realtor.

I could see Haden was excited about moving. I still wasn't on board, but I could see I was going to be outvoted when I saw everyone nodding gently and scanning each other for objections. I didn't like the idea of sleeping in a home I could never have afforded in my real life, because I knew it would never feel like my home.

"The next house is a mile away, but the next neighborhood of houses is only three miles away," I pointed out. Haden's face fell and I could see she hadn't thought about that. It was a little too close for comfort and she knew it.

"How many?" Garrett asked.

I tried to mentally picture the neighborhood. "At least eight, I think. Big ones."

"Lots of space between them?" he asked.

"Yeah, like an acre," I answered. Garrett looked to Devin. They were silently discussing something with perked eyebrows and shrugs. Haden cheered up as she looked between them. "What?" I asked, missing the boat on the conversation subtitles.

"We could clear out the houses," Garrett said. "There can't be more than six people per house. Fifty total." His mouth tangled in contemplation. "We could do doubles, with Priest as our lookout. We could clear them all out in one night, assuming I'm overestimating."

Everyone was in agreement, except me. My instincts weren't screaming at me the way they did when August was in danger, but I was very aware of my desire to run away.

Belongings

IN THE GRAND SCHEME of things, belongings mean nothing. Clothing is simply a method of protecting your skin and staying warm. If they actually fit then you were ahead of the curve. A quick look at my closet told me there wasn't much worth taking with me. I packed one bag to make it through the first few days without doing laundry.

Trinkets and ornaments were useless and a waste of space. Sentimentality did nothing to change that fact. Scanning my room, I could see the many dolls that were once precious to Nicole. I imagined she would have had trouble walking away from them, but to me they meant nothing. The only reason they hadn't been thrown out was out of respect for her. Plus, there wasn't exactly garbage service anymore.

The quilt on the bed was the only thing I was remotely interested in taking. It was shabby and old and reminded me of something my mother might have put on my bed as a child. Still, it wasn't my name on the quilt. The sentimentality I thought I was feeling was from another owner.

With my tote bag of clothes in hand, I headed to the bathroom to gather what I needed there. The only necessary personal items post-apocalypse, besides clothing, were deodorant and toothpaste. No one wants a toothache in this world. Dental work now consisted of pliers and two strong friends: one strong enough to hold you down and one strong enough not to pass out before they got your tooth out.

The new house would already be furnished with our other necessities: furniture, cooking tools, towels, and bedding. The only thing left to do when we arrived was air out the fridge, divvy up the rooms, and kill some grim.

I handed my bag to Priest and he loaded it in the back of his SUV. Devin and Haden had already left in the Dodge with Garrett's motorcycle loaded in the back. I couldn't help but look out over the old cornfields toward the cemetery where August was buried. "We should go see her before we leave. Who knows when we'll get back this way again?"

Priest frowned at me. "Is that why you've been so reluctant to leave here? You don't want to be so far away from her?"

I shrugged. "I have a laundry list of reasons not to leave here. All of them end in me stomping my feet and pouting, though, so there's no need to bring them up."

"You're allowed your opinion," he said.

"Everyone else wants a new house. Besides, we are kind of on top of each other in this place."

Priest nodded, glancing back at the house where Garrett was still loading up some food so we didn't have to restock right away. "You know, you don't have to do things to make other people happy. Not if it makes you unhappy."

"What's that supposed to mean?" I bristled.

Priest sighed. "Something's changed with you and him. I can see it. You aren't happy being with him. Not that you were ever a fountain of joy in his presence, but now you seem numb around him, like you're playing a part."

"What's your point?" I pushed my bag in a little more for something to do.

Priest looked behind me as the screen door slammed against the house on Garrett's exit. He lowered his voice. "You don't need to stay with him just to make him happy."

"Are you offering anything better?" I snarled, matching his volume.

"Lenore." He frowned, but he didn't make an offer.

"Then don't worry about it. I'm happier with him than alone."

"Little help," Garrett hollered as he came up. Priest met up with him and took a box off the top of his pile and loaded it. "What are you two cavorting about?" he asked, putting the boxes in.

"Lenore was thinking about visiting August before we headed up to the house," Priest said. "I wasn't sure if you would be ready for that or not." Garrett looked at him a moment before responding.

"Actually, I wouldn't be." Garrett shook his head and looked back at me somberly. "I'm sorry, Lenore, I don't think I could. Not yet, anyway."

I frowned sympathetically and nodded. I wasn't about to push a man, who had seen so much loss in his life, to aggravate his grief further. "I understand."

"Do we have everything we need?" Priest asked, shutting the back.

"Everything worth keeping, anyway." Garrett smiled and pulled me over to him by the waist. It was sweet, and I of course gave him my best smile for his effort. Priest wasn't the only one who knew my heart wasn't in it, but since no other offer was on the table, my heart would continue to belong to me.

More

"I FOUND THE PLACE. *Of course* I should get the master bed-room." Haden and Devin were already fighting by the time we made it to the house. Priest, Garrett, and I each dumped our boxes of food in the kitchen and waited for the decision to be made.

"Oh, I don't think so." Devin crossed his arms in a less than playful display. "You can't just bully your way to get what you want."

"Why don't you two share it?" I asked. "You practically spend every night together anyway."

The double glare that came from them was enough to make me retreat from the fight altogether. Apparently, Devin and Haden were still not willing to devote themselves to each other permanently.

"Night or not, I need my space and my options." Haden perked her brow at Devin and he narrowed his eyes at her.

"So do I," he agreed.

"I hate to point this out," Priest said as he leaned back on the railing separating the high kitchen from the living room, "but this house has four bedrooms and there are five of us. Two people are going to have to share a room. If you two want separate rooms, then it's only fair the couple sharing a room should get the larger room." Silence ensued that was both threatening and thoughtful. "So, I guess that settles it. Garret and I will take the master bedroom." Priest stepped over to Garrett and rested his arm over his shoulders. It took a moment for the joke to draw laughter, but once it did, the tension in the room started to lift.

"I should warn you, I'm a cuddler," Garrett surprisingly added to the joke.

"Well, I guess that's only fair," Devin said. "Privacy or luxury, I'll take privacy."

"You're happy with anything, as long as I don't have more than you," Haden scolded.

"Damn straight." Devin picked up his bag and headed toward the far rooms. "Dibs on the front window!" he yelled as he started to sprint. Haden ran after him screaming profanities.

Priest sighed. "I'm going to go point out that their lovemaking sessions will be far easier to tolerate with a hallway between them and me. Doubtful they'll care." He rolled his eyes before heading back.

I wasn't sure why Priest had pushed for Garrett and me to get the master bedroom, especially given our recent conversation, but I imagined it was for the same reason he wanted the front bedroom sharing a wall with the bathrooms—he wanted as many walls as possible between him and us.

I started unloading the groceries and Garrett approached me from behind, wrapping his hands around me before slipping one into my pants. My breath caught and I leaned against him. He may not have had my heart, but my body was still very receptive to him. "Is that okay?"

"Yes," I said breathlessly as he massaged his fingers over me.

"No, I mean the room. We haven't spoken much about... that topic. Are you still comfortable with me being so close to you?" He pushed a finger inside of me as he finished the question. He could have been asking me to scrub a toilet and I would have said yes to him.

I was dimly aware this was his way of staying close to me. Had he simply asked the question independent of his manipulation I might have been prone to express my real opinion on being with him. Now that I was preoccupied, the only answer I could think of was, "Yes."

"Good."

To my dismay he removed his hand from my pants. Instead he spun me around and threw me over his shoulder like a sack of potatoes. With his free hand he scooped up our bags and shuffled off to the master bedroom.

He tossed the luggage—me included—on the bed before he closed and locked the door. I was surprised to find he didn't slow his advance when we were alone. He didn't bother undressing either of us. He just unzipped his pants to release himself.

My pants at least made it to my ankles, before he rammed inside of me slightly painfully but with purpose. I half yelped, half moaned and he gently pressed his hand over my mouth. "I don't want to share your pleasure with anyone anymore. I want it all for my ears," he whispered as he rhythmically pushed against me.

He shoved my shirt and bra up enough to grab and suckle my breasts. I could barely contain my audible enthusiasm as he made me climax faster than I anticipated. When I was spent he continued to push me on until I had no energy left to climax. "Stop please."

"Don't you want more?" he asked, panting on top of me. "I can go longer."

"No." I shook my head, pushing back tears. "No, I don't want more." He finished and rolled off of me. He hastily escaped into the restroom to wash up before I could express the sentiments he had avoided by pushing me into bed in the first place.

Other Than the Love Stuff

UNPACKING TOOK ALL OF about three minutes. Exploring my new wardrobe took another hour. Most of the master bedroom clothes were office apparel for the lady of the house, but she did have a few t-shirts and jeans that fit me well enough with a belt.

Emerging from the bedroom, I found Devin, Garret, and Priest huddled around the coffee table in the living room. Haden was putting together a snack in our new kitchen. She apparently found a room formerly belonging to a teenage girl. She had no qualms about wearing the tight-fitting vintage t-shirts and hoodies, despite the fashion being too young for her.

"I can shoot a gun. I'm not completely useless," Priest insisted.

"Haden?" Devin asked without turning around. He caught sight of me, smiled and ushered me over to him.

"He's a decent enough shot," Haden answered back.

"Did you get settled in fine?" Devin asked, drawing his arm around me as I sat next to him on the couch. Priest looked me over, but drew his eyes back to the makeshift map Devin had drawn up of the neighborhood we planned to evacuate tonight.

The map was reminiscent of a Candy Land board game with its bright crayon roads and stick houses with the house numbers over the top. Devin's plan was simple: take the outer houses first and work our way in. We didn't want to get trapped or bombarded, so we needed a lookout. Priest was arguing against it being him, but he wasn't making a lot of progress.

"When we get to the last few, you can go inside," Devin said flatly. "Bottom line, we need someone outside. Since you're a nice shooter, you won't be useless. Believe me, there's bound to be a few around the area to make your watch worth while."

Priest seemed disheartened by his meager role, but surrendered the fight and leaned back in his chair. Haden shoved a tray of sandwiches in my face. I smiled and took one as she continued to hand them out. The bread had been frozen judging by its texture, but any baked good made for a happy meal.

"I could stay outside," I suggested over a mouth full of sandwich.

"Lenore," Garrett scolded, misinterpreting my proposal as cowardice. "You are perfectly capable of doing this." I glared at him for the condescension.

"Arrows are a better open-space weapon. We all know I can't hit the side of a barn with a gun. If Priest can shoot, he'd be a better ally in close quarters than someone who has to reload with every shot."

"Good point," Devin said, consulting nonverbally with Haden before continuing. "You want him or Garrett?" he asked her.

It was starting to sound like gym class, picking the best player for your team. Garrett and Priest watched Haden contemplate, eager to find out who their partner would be. "Hmm," she pondered aloud while she rubbed her hands together, "which one of you will annoy me less?" She posed the question without an ounce of humor.

"Oh, just choose," Garrett rebuked her.

"Okay, Matthew." She narrowed her eyes at Garrett.

"Thank you, Haden," Priest said with a gloating tone. "I look forward to watching your ass." He grinned at her as she stood up. She scowled, but eventually gave him a smile for the joke. It made me smile too, even though I didn't like seeing him flirt with another woman.

Haden headed back into the kitchen for a drink, and Devin glanced after her before speaking. "Seriously Matthew," he said, "anything happens to her and it's your head."

Priest gave him a nod that was almost a bow.

Whether he realized it or not, Devin had tightened his grip on me to a level just shy of pain. I cleared my throat to draw his attention back to me and he let up rubbing my arm after he did. "You ready for this?" he asked.

I wanted to say no. I wanted to tell him I was nervous about what was going to happen, but I also knew that battles like this were inevitable. We needed to stay in practice. We needed to keep the grim under control. Not to mention, we needed to get our egos checked. If for no other reason than that, I kept my reservations quiet. "Ready as I'll ever be."

And I'll Raise You

THE PERIMETER SEARCH CONSISTED of a painstakingly slow and stealthy walk around the back of the neighborhood, which was a tiny creek lined with trees. Garrett and Devin had stayed posted by the road in opposite corners while Haden, Priest, and I took successive positions to stalk through the tall grasses and alert them via flashlight of signs of grim, which they likewise would do for us.

Haden was ahead of me, and Priest was not far behind me. The nights were still cold and it didn't appear that warmth would be making a comeback anytime soon. I could see my breath, which told me we were already being stupid. Grim didn't breathe, so they could be standing behind trees three feet away and we wouldn't see them, but they would see us no matter how well we hid.

I hissed up to Haden, but she didn't hear me. I looked back at Priest and caught his attention. I pointed to my exhaled breath and dangled my scarf. I wrapped it around my mouth and he nodded and did likewise.

There were lights on in all the houses, simply because no one ever bothered to go house to house and shut the electricity off. So far, someone was still keeping us in power and we were thankful for it.

I pulled out my binoculars and looked into the windows of the nearest house. There was no movement inside. Through the upstairs window I could see the reflection of the room in a vanity mirror. A woman's body hung from a ceiling fan.

I pulled the binoculars away and didn't bother perusing the rest of the houses. "What is it?" Priest whispered. He had closed much of the distance between us.

"Nothing, just some *day tens*," I said.

"You seem on edge," he pointed out.

"Yeah, well..." I didn't know how to answer him. The truth was probably best. "Priest, you're going to have to watch your back tonight. This isn't going to be pretty."

"What do you mean? What are you feeling?"

"I'm feeling *on edge*," I said sardonically. "I don't feel like running, but I do feel like being vigilant."

"You think we're walking into a trap?" His eyes widened.

"No. If I did, I would be jumping out of my skin. I think we can handle whatever is in store for us, but I think we are being damn sloppy."

"Then tell Devin and Haden," he said simply.

"They don't want me telling them what to do."

"I'm sure they respect you enough to listen to your concerns, and if they don't, make them. They can hardly resent you if you keep them from getting killed."

"Actually, they can, because they would be alive to resent me. You don't understand. I can't replace August. It would be... disrespectful to take her place, no matter what I promised her."

"Wait, what did you promise August?"

I sighed. My can of worms was spilling everywhere and the little buggers were squirming away too fast to put back in. "Before August died in my arms, she made me promise to take care of them, to take her place and lead them."

"Oh, Lenore." Priest frowned. "You have to do as she wished."

"Don't talk to me about dying wishes. She overestimated me once. I won't let her do it again, posthumously or otherwise." I started to move away, but Priest pulled my arm practically toppling me with the abrupt direction change.

"No, Lenore, this isn't about dying wishes. This is about her giving you your purpose. She may have overestimated you, but only because she didn't want to die. You are underestimating yourself. You should be leading this team."

"Fuck off, how would you know?" I tried to shrug him away, but he grabbed my collar. I slipped on the slick grass, unable to get purchase. I needed to fend him off without outright punching him—which I hadn't ruled out yet.

"I know, because August knew and I trust her judgment."

"Since when?" I said louder than I intended.

"Since..." He froze and stared blankly at me. He either, didn't have an answer or he didn't want to share his answer. He shook his head. "You trusted her enough to become a fighter. Why would you not trust her enough to become a leader?"

"Because I can't do it," I rasped, trying to keep my volume under control.

Priest growled and shook me by my coat collar. "You *are* doing it!" He was still whispering as well, but with the vehemence of yelling. "But you aren't speaking up. You know when something's not right.

Damn it, Lenore, you always talk about doing what feels right, but you aren't doing that. You're fighting your instincts tooth and nail, because you're too much of an abdicator to contradict your friends! For once in your fucking life, say what you need to say!"

"You want me to speak up?" I clutched his collar much like he was mine. "Fine! I love you!"

The sentiment fell between us as gracefully as a brick. His eyes widened. He wasn't expecting a confession of love to be my first order of business. I was a little floored by it myself, but as soon as I said it I knew it was true. He let go of me and distanced himself. His lapels tugged from my grasp as he did. Various emotions were filtering through his expression, but he didn't voice any of them.

"I'm not the only one fighting my instincts around here, am I?" I snarled with resuscitated umbrage at his rejection.

"Hey!" Haden hissed from ahead of us. "Shut your racket and get moving. I want to be done by sunrise!" I waved her off and turned back to Priest, who still looked shaken.

"Lenore, I—"

"Just forget it! I don't want to hear another speech about how much you feel, but can't act on. I would rather go back to when you thought I was repugnant. At least I understood that. Would have hurt a lot less, too." I walked away and I could hear him follow, but he didn't make any attempts to catch up. Nothing had changed, not even with a second "I love you" ante in the pot.

A New Sheriff in Candy Land

INSPIRED BY—OR IN SPITE of—my conversation with Priest, I decided I did need to speak up. Even if I didn't want to be the leader, I at least needed to be a team player, and that involved having the ball once in a while.

"Okay, let's split up," Devin ordered when we were all back at the neighborhood entrance.

"No," I said flatly, without any particular opening for questions behind it. "We need to take these first two houses together." Devin looked at me strangely, as did Haden and Garrett, but I didn't stop to wait for a vote. "These are the nicest houses in town. If they weren't swarming with grim, then someone would have taken over this neighborhood by now. Not everyone is as frugal as we are."

"That sounds reasonable," Devin agreed. "Did you just think of that, or did you forget to raise your hand at the meeting earlier." I ignored the undertone of sarcasm.

"We'll go in through the garages, quietly if possible. Steal gas from the vehicles or snag the flammable chemicals on the shelves and start the living room on fire. We don't go in the basement, and we don't go upstairs. We get out once it's good and blazing and wait for the buggers to burn or flee like roaches. What the fire doesn't finish off we shoot ourselves. Assuming we aren't completely bombarded, we can roast marshmallows between houses."

Haden and Devin exchanged looks, but didn't seem to have any major objections to my plan other than it not being their plan. Priest had a smirk on his face. He looked like he was proud of me. It was annoying, to say the least.

"Alright, Plan B, belated but in effect." Devin pulled out his lighter and flicked the flame on. "Good thing I smoke." He winked and I smiled.

Asses to Ashes

I GRABBED A GALLON of paint thinner while the others si-
phoned some gas from the cars. I stepped inside the house and
tiptoed through the mudroom and into the kitchen. As I rounded
the corner to the living room I saw a body on the couch. I barely
got a view of the blood and brains splattered on the wall behind
the slumped-over corpse before I ducked back behind the wall.

I had to remind myself that grim rarely used decayed flesh as
vessels. Suicide victims were at least spared that indignity.

I came back around breathing through my mouth, and desperately trying not to look directly at the body. No luck on my
side—there were three more bodies on the adjacent love seat. By
the looks of it, a mother and two children, each with their very
own head wound. Murder-suicide.

I tried not to think how hard it would be to kill your own family
out of mercy. I tried not to think about a lot of things.

I poured the paint thinner over the bodies and the couches. The
others joined me, pouring gasoline into the carpet and splashing
it onto the curtains. With the exception of the jostled liquids, we
were soundless.

Devin looked to me for the go ahead and I nodded. We all headed back through the kitchen toward the garage. Devin stopped at the kitchen table and lit a bundle of napkins on fire with his lighter. He tossed them into the living room and jumped back when the room erupted with more zeal than he expected.

We all ran away from the house and lined up on the road out front to watch it burn. Devin laughed and butted me in the shoulder with his. "This is way more fun. Good idea, Lenore."

I was about to jokingly comment on my former life as an amateur pyromaniac, but the screeching grim crashing out of the upstairs window threw me off. Haden wasn't taken by surprise. She downed the creature before it was fully erect.

I readied my bow, but nothing else happened. I was starting to wonder if I had been too paranoid about the dangers in this neighborhood. Naturally, I lowered my weapon. That seemingly logical choice drew the attention of the ever-present Murphy's Law.

"Holy shit!" Haden shifted position, heading toward the second house. "They're coming from the southeast side!"

We followed Haden until we could see around the house. A horde of grim were charging at us. The third house in had been infested with them. The area *had* been a trap. Anyone coming to claim the immaculate homes would have been overtaken the minute they got comfortable inside.

Haden started firing and I shot my arrows in quick succession. Unfortunately, the grim were old—and fast. They weren't easily troubled by my body shots.

As with any specialized weaponry, there were pitfalls depending on the opponent. I switched to my gun and managed to hit a few, probably because there were so many. "Fall back!" Devin yelled and we all stepped back, giving us more time before we had to resort to hand-to-hand combat.

Despite being capable of bare-knuckle battles, I still preferred to avoid it. The less contact I had with the grim, the better, in my opinion.

Contrary to everyone else, Priest moved forward instead of back. I glanced to Garrett on my left. "What the hell is he doing?" I asked.

"Matthew! Get back!" Garrett rumbled.

Priest didn't stop. He proceeded into our line of fire and into the path of the grim. Haden moved forward to pull him back, but the distraction left her open. One grim charged ahead of the group, bypassed Priest, and grabbed her neck. Her trigger clicked impotently. She was out of bullets.

Priest reached back and grabbed the attacking grim by the neck. It squealed like a frightened rabbit and fell stiffly to the ground. The remaining grim slowed their attack, steering clear of Priest. Haden reloaded and took out another half dozen before I could switch back to my bow in hopes of providing some accurate help.

Devin and Garrett fought off two that had reached us. A third arrived in time for me to try out my hunting knife. It wasn't my preferred weapon, but I was willing to try anything that didn't require good aim.

Its skull split like a melon and part of it toppled away in a bloodless trail of sandy residue. Devin punched the final attacker that was coming right at me. He shattered its head like a confetti balloon all over me. I spat the crystallized human remains off my lips and shook my hair out. Devin helped dust off my clothes, smiling at my discomfort.

"What the hell did you do to that thing?" Haden danced around the grim Priest had dropped with a single touch. She kicked it, but it didn't move. She looked to Priest, but he didn't offer much. As with any new unnatural skill, it wasn't a prerequisite to understand it. "Did you freeze it? Knock it out? What?"

"I think I removed the demon," Priest said.

"Since when can you do that?" Haden pitched.

"Since now, I guess," he responded, seeming just as surprised by the skill.

"Crap-appaloosa, could we get the crib notes on you two freaks, so we aren't—"

"We are not freaks!" Priest bellowed at her with unfamiliar venom.

Haden looked to me, unsure of what button she had pushed. I assumed it was either the same nerve that made him hate the word 'crazy,' or he didn't like that she had lumped me into the category with him. I just shook my head at her.

"Whatever," she said, sounding slightly calmer. "Is it possible for you two to get your superhero powers figured out before you get one of us killed with your experiments?"

"You mean like practice?" I asked.

"Yeah." Haden nodded and pinned her hands on her hips. "You two are both running on autopilot with big question marks in your eyes. You need to start figuring out what the hell you're doing and start taking the reins."

"Just to be clear," Devin interjected, "are they flying a plane or riding a horse?" I bit back my smile, but Haden gave us both a glare.

"I'm serious," Haden wailed and I couldn't help but snort at how vehement she was being. "Oh, screw you two jackasses." She stormed away while Devin and I continued to snicker.

Once we were contained, Devin turned to me and smiled broadly. "That was a good plan. We would have been sitting ducks in that house." I nodded. "You were very forceful too. It was hot." He looked me up and down. I smiled, shying away from his gaze even though I knew he was teasing me. "Do you know what I would like to do with you, right here, right now?" he whispered seductively.

I laughed. "I bet it's something *hot*."

"Oh, yeah." He flipped out his lighter. "Burn baby burn." He ran toward the next house and I followed, leaving Garrett and Priest to either find some marshmallows and join in, or wallow with Haden.

The Dangers of Being Humane

THE LAST HOUSE WAS a good deal smaller. It was probably the first house on the land and by way of keeping up with the Jones's, every successive house had gotten bigger. By rights, it was probably better off burnt down, judging by the damage to the outside. The windows were broken out and the siding had been ripped off.

Devin and I came up to the acreage with the same cautious approach we did the other houses, even though the last two houses appeared to be vacant. This one, however, deserved more caution, since the smoke stack was billowing smoke. There was one light on upstairs.

"How should we do this one?" Devin asked. "The garage is separate. Front or back door?"

"Wait." I grabbed his arm and ducked down. He immediately joined me, pulling his gun and waving a stop to Garrett who was coming up from behind in case we found trouble. Priest had stayed behind to apologize to Haden. I didn't think it would take so long, but she must have had a few more beefs to rattle off while we were burning down potentially grim-filled houses. However, I wasn't one to judge the timing of topics.

"Something isn't right," I said. "Why would grim need a fire-place?" I pulled out my binoculars to get a closer look at the house.

The windows on the lower floor were broken, but plywood panels were blocking them from the inside. The upstairs windows were intact. The north bedroom was dark, but the light from the hall provided enough illumination to reveal the endless boxes of canned food.

"This is a squatter house, not a grim hold," I said, scanning to the south window. "Wait." In the lit bedroom I could see a woman lying on a bed. She was asleep or dead. Her skin had a familiar sheen. "There's a grim in there. Why would—?"

The woman's eyes opened and her head turned. She looked out the window… at me. I pulled the binoculars away, disturbed by the connection. It reminded me of how Adrian Dorn always knew when I was watching him. Devin looked at me, obviously curious of my sudden retraction, but didn't ask.

I raised the binoculars and looked back at the room. The grim smiled at me, before riling into soundless snarls and screams. She bared her teeth, lurching to get at me even though I was nearly a hundred yards away. If she was sensing my presence from so far away, she must have been very old. Or the demon inside her was very strong.

She struggled against the handcuffs around her wrists. The metal restraints were carving into her fossilized skin.

The door to the room opened and a man came in, rushing to her side. She was momentarily distracted by him and tried to bite him as he attempted to press her down. His forearms had more than a few bandages. He pursed his lips, shushing her and petting her hair back, all the while avoiding her teeth.

She turned her attention back to the window and snarled at my presence. The man moved to a different part of the room, out of view of the window. He reappeared a moment later with a rifle and looked out the window. He scanned the perimeter outside for the cause of his grim's sudden fit.

I pulled the binoculars away from my eyes and looked down at the frosty grass. Life after the apocalypse was complicated, but this was a glimpse into a psychosis level of denial. I could only presume the grim was the man's wife. I imagine he believed she was still in there somewhere, just being consumed by a passing disease. It was whatever he told himself, and not one of us was going to convince him he was wrong.

"What is it?" Devin reached for the binoculars and I pulled them away. He narrowed his eyes, insulted by my hoarding.

"Please, don't. You know the movies that leave you feeling sad and kind of icky at the end?" Understanding started to reach his eyes. "That's all you'll get from looking in that house. We can leave it. Trust me, that house isn't a danger to anyone."

Not Again

BY THE TIME WE made it back to the house, everyone had fallen into the silence that comes with being too tired to care about the silence. Priest parked the SUV in the driveway. Haden and Devin got out and did a perimeter sweep before we got settled in for the night.

Garrett and I headed in and he went straight to the master bedroom. He glanced back at me when I didn't come. "You coming?"

"Yeah, I just need to see if Devin can handle the watch." He didn't seem to trust that it was my real reason for lagging, but he didn't try to persuade me to do otherwise. He disappeared into the room as Priest came in the front.

Our eyes met and I started to say something in the way of an apology, but the back door opened and Haden stepped inside. "Devin said he'll finish up the night on watch, as long as someone is awake by seven."

"I'll set my alarm," Priest offered. "I'm an early bird anyway."

"Did you talk to her?" Haden asked, nodding to me.

Priest shook his head. "I just walked in."

"Matthew thinks he might be able to become an asset to our little group as a grim exterminator." She crossed her arms like she still wasn't sure she believed him.

"I'm not entirely sure, but given tonight..." He looked at me. "I think there is room to hope I won't be completely useless to you guys after all."

"You aren't useless," I mumbled, heading into the kitchen for a glass of water.

"I want him to practice his ability," Haden said.

I looked back at her. "What, on grim? I suppose we could go door to door, but that's a close proximity skill, it's going to be kind of dangerous."

Haden nodded. "Yeah, but necessary." She glanced at Priest like she was consulting with him before speaking. "I think you should practice your ability too."

I nearly choked on my water. I cleared my throat and turned to her. "I read evil, what's to practice?"

Priest stepped forward. "We were discussing how Dorn was able to deceive you until I interrupted and disrupted whatever hold he had on you. We were also discussing your vision." I looked away from both of them. "Haden thinks if your skills were honed you might be able to see past Dorn's... fantasy, and see his ultimate plan."

"What if his fantasy *is* his ultimate plan?" I said, turning back to them. "What if he's a sick freak who wants to cut and burn me while he fucks me?"

Haden stepped forward, bypassing conversational distance to stand right in front of me. "I don't think August died so he could get into your pants. You know he is more than a sicko." She was right about that, but I hadn't allowed my mind to delve into the possibilities surrounding Adrian Dorn. "If he's got fr—special powers like you two, we need to be able to bypass them. If he is planning something, then we need to know what it is and stop it."

"What if he's too strong for us to defeat? What if—?"

"We aren't in the business of what ifs. August didn't drag me out of a gutter and nurse me back to health because she wanted a roommate. She did it because she wanted to fight the evil threatening to take over the Earth. She chose me because I'm determined as hell and she knew I would keep this team driven long after her death, which means kicking your stubborn ass when necessary."

I hadn't heard much about Haden's past, but I knew she considered herself permanently indebted to August. I could only assume the reference to the gutter was not a euphemism.

"Starting tomorrow you are back in training," she commanded. I groaned at hearing that word again, but Haden ignored me. "I want you sniffing out evil, reading every naughty little grim thought, and whatever else you can pull out of that hat trick you call a brain. Got it?"

I was aware Haden was using this opportunity to regain her authority over me since I had virtually taken over the attack earlier, but she was right to demand more of me.

I had taken my new skill for granted when I went up against Dorn the last time. I assumed it would be easy to read his mind and unravel his dastardly plan, but I was wrong. If anything, I had played right into his hand and that wasn't good. My instincts were good, but in the end, I still needed to know my opponent's plan, or my instincts would leave me falling short, just like they did with August.

"I'll start looking for some evildoers tomorrow," I agreed and headed off to bed. I still wanted to talk to Priest, but the moment of convenient solitude was gone, and I was tired. Once again I was slipping off to bed with Garrett after an "I love you" had been dropped between Priest and me.

Down the Rabbit Hole

I MAGES OF THE STANDARD carnage ran through my mind: rape, murder, body mutilation, and cannibalism. I was becoming immune to most of it. I hardly ever puked anymore.

I released the grim Devin and Garrett were holding for me and shrugged. I had nothing new to offer them. If there were any deep thoughts in demons, it wasn't coming through on my end.

Priest came in behind me with the same hat trick, but instead he imparted his thoughts to the grim. Not such a scary proposal, until you experience firsthand his ability to funnel in a few choice insights from the Big Guy himself. The imperious power emanating from him was palpable. Even Garrett and Devin shied away from watching his process close up.

Priest could make the grim squeal and screech with one touch. How long the agony lasted was apparently up to him. One particular grim had kicked me in the face prior to my reading and Priest made squeal for nearly a minute before it went stiff. This one however, was gone with one yelp.

"At least this bullshit is helping one of us," I commented after Garrett and Devin laid the grim body down in the grass. The last few nights of grim hunting had been exhausting to me. I had expected to delve into the complex minds of demons, but thus far the grim had been as much puppets on the inside as they were on the outside. Maim, defile, kill, and repeat.

"Maybe we should get older ones," Garrett suggested.

"It was hard enough to catch the young ones," Devin objected. "You would think grim wouldn't run from four heavily armed living people. What is the world coming to?"

I smiled at Devin's joke, even though Garrett was already annoyed at me for not taking this training seriously. Naturally, he was on Haden's side and had made it his personal goal to get me into mental shape, just as he had gotten me into physical shape.

"Touch it again," Priest said, standing over the grim pensively.

"Why? He's finito. Muerto," I said. Priest stared at me, making no further argument for his request other than being him.

I lolled my head back in weary annoyance, but I leaned down to the body and touched it with dramatic sarcasm. I expected to see the same horrible images or nothing, but instead down the rabbit hole and into hell I went.

The rushing sensation was as near a rollercoaster as I'd ever been. An expanse of minds unfolded before me. The river of sorrow threading through my mind was a welcome relief to the shifting dizzying thoughts of hundreds or thousands of angry minds. The agony of loss, abandonment, and guilt fueled the anger that was suffocating my own thoughts.

Within it all, I could feel something hungry. I was drawn to that core energy much like I was drawn to evil. *So hungry*. Starving despite the endless amount of pain feeding it. I knew it would never be satisfied. It would hunger long after the human race had been extinguished, because it was hungry long before we arrived.

I felt myself being pulled and I resisted. I screamed from the rage pounding into my mind. I wanted it to stop, but I also couldn't let go of it. I wanted to be angry. I wanted to get a front row seat to yell at whoever was responsible for all this chaos. Most of all, I wanted them to suffer and if the only way I could do that was by hurting myself, then so be it.

The Art of Zen

GARRETT BLOCKED ME FROM lunging at Priest. For once, his stoic face actually showed concern for my well-being. I clawed his face as punishment for the intervention, and he punched me in the stomach. I recoiled enough to make him follow and I elbowed him in the face.

Priest watched us with fascination, but no particular sympathy. He knew what he was sending me into and he didn't even warn me. I was furious at him for sending me there, and furious at Devin and Garrett for pulling me out.

"You son of a bitch!" I went after Priest again while Garrett was distracted, but Devin lassoed me around the waist with a tight grip. He wasn't as strong as Garret, but his moves were quick and decisive. He lifted me before I could gain purchase, and wrestled me down again, awkwardly kneeling behind me, pinning my calves under his knees.

"Lenore, stop," he pleaded, hugging me to his chest. I wanted to calm down. I knew I was being irrational, but I couldn't let it go. I wanted to get back at Priest. I wanted to hurt him.

"I hate you! You pompous, heartless prick! How can you just stand there like nothing has happened?"

"Let her go, Devin," Priest said calmly.

"Are you fucking kidding me?" his voice pitched.

"If you let me go, I'll kill him!" I raged with no sign of exaggeration in my tone. "Did you know where that would take me, or were you just using me as a guinea pig? Again!"

"What the hell happened to you, Lenore?" Devin asked, but Priest seemed to be interested in the answer as well.

"I caught a glimpse of hell, and maybe, just maybe, the senior advisor too." I bucked my head back, slamming my head into Devin. He released his grip to cradle his face and I elbowed him in the gut.

His reaction wasn't as I anticipated and I found myself flattened to the ground with my arm painfully close to dislocating at the shoulder joint. "Don't forget who you're fighting, baby," he whispered in my ear like he didn't want to have to prove his combat skills to me again.

I screamed into the dirt, unable to move without excruciating pain. I laid out a long list of expletives, but none of them made me feel better. I could see Priest kneel next to me and I struggled to get at him.

"Wait, what are you going to do?" Devin asked.

"I'm going to relieve her mind," Priest told him.

"Don't you fucking touch me you self-affirmed eunuch! Devin, let me go!"

"In a minute, baby. Let's try Matthew's way first." He brushed my hair back behind my ear. I was impressed he could maintain his gentle nature even while he was crushing me into the ground.

"This *is* his way! Throw me at the problem and see what happens," I ranted. "He's just like the rest of you. I'm one of August's tools to all of you. I could leave tomorrow and the only reason anyone would come looking for me is because of August."

"That's not true, Lenore," I heard Garrett say behind me somewhere, but I couldn't move my head enough to see him.

"You especially, Garrett. I'm just a pit stop for your dick! Go back to your fucking wife!" I sensed the shift in attention as Priest and Devin questioned my admission, but I was too busy in my rage dance to care what gossip I had ignited. "Don't you all get it? She's dead! You don't have to keep pretending to care about saving the world."

"Just let Matthew do whatever voodoo he wants." Garrett gave his irritated consent. "Anything to shut her up."

"Release her," Priest ordered Devin.

"Leave me alone! Go back to your harem, Priest! At least you were interesting as a belligerent drunk."

Devin pulled me up and tethered me against his chest. "Do whatever you need to, but I'm not leaving her side."

Priest repositioned in front of me. "You may regret that choice, but I won't argue." Priest leaned forward and pressed his hands to my face. I closed my eyes, preparing for whatever he was going to do to me.

"No!" I screamed at him. The anger I felt may have been seeded by my own, but something else had bloomed it into this rage. And I liked it. It felt good to be mad. It felt good to yell, and I wasn't ready to stop.

I felt the warmth penetrating me from his hands and I fought against it, hanging onto the anger and the pain that inevitably rooted it to me.

"Lenore, don't fight me," Priest said, feeling the shifting war over my mind.

"Fuck you," I ground out. "This is my mind! You don't control me and neither does He!"

"We'll see how far free will gets you," he said, curling his fingers in my hair. Tentacles of calm reached my mind. The anger was too splintered to hang onto. Instead, I reached past it, deep beyond my logical, emotional mind, to my inner strength, what I imagined to be my soul. It unfurled inside of me pushing liquid courage and pure vigor into my veins. When I heard Priest gasp, I couldn't help but smile.

"Lenore, what is that?" he asked.

"I don't know, but it feels pretty good." I laughed. I sounded maniacal. I was pleased as punch to be stronger than Priest, mentally at least.

"Devin, let her go. You don't want to be part of this," Priest warned, but Devin wouldn't budge. "Let go of it, Lenore. Whatever this is, you're not ready for it. Stop it now!" I waited for the please, but it didn't come. "Or I'll stop it for you."

"Just try it," I goaded him.

"I'm sorry, Lenore." I expected the same slow as molasses flowing warmth, but it wasn't him this time. Along with a sudden ignition inside of me, I could feel a lottery of emotions, but they were all in the background. The only dominant sensation was power, but not mine and not Priest's. It pressed down on me, physically and mentally, demanding in no small way my complete and utter submission. In the face of such an awesome display my courage evaporated. I felt as insignificant as an ant to a shoe.

Yet, somehow, even cowering as I did beneath the grandiose nature of the encounter, I didn't feel subjugated. I felt important and loved, albeit scolded on a cosmic level. Why I was loved, I didn't understand.

Powerless, I let go of my guilt, my resentment, and my loneliness. My mind and heart were a platter, and from it the waste was cleaned and the burdens ripped from me as if I had no right to be holding onto them to begin with. I was temporarily a blank slate that any seeker of Zen would have envied. It may have only been for a moment, but it was a great moment.

Oops

W HEN I WAS AWARE of my surroundings again. Priest was gone and Devin was holding me to his chest, but I got the impression it wasn't to keep me still anymore. I turned to look at him and I saw tears streaming from his reddened eyes.

I could only presume his proximity to me left him open to backlash from my emotional exorcism. If seeing was believing, then feeling was understanding, and I knew from experience how scary that was the first time around.

I wiped away one of his tears and he leaned down and hugged me closer. "You okay?" I asked.

"Yeah, I feel a little violated, but in a good way." He chuckled and pulled away from me. "This stuff is getting pretty intense."

"Yeah, I guess so." I wasn't sure what to say to him. Being face to face with the power Priest tapped into was as belittling as it was enlightening. Not to mention whatever I had tapped into on my own.

Despite being a part of what had just happened, I didn't understand it any more than Devin did. The new power I had discovered intimidated Priest enough to pull out the big guns to stop it. It was, of course, no match for his former boss, but then again, what power would be? The only thing I knew for sure was I owed apologies all around.

I made my apologies to Devin even though I hadn't hurt him with anything personal. He promptly forgave me and apologized for his brutish behavior, even though it was wholly warranted for him to gruffly subdue any woman with hell-infused PMS. He gave me a kiss that wasn't nearly as wet as the ones he used to give me, but still not so chaste that I wouldn't recognize his lips.

We got up and dusted the threads of new grass off ourselves. The spring had finally arrived ready to ease us into another hot summer. For once in my life, I was enjoying the bitter cold winter. To see it go only reminded me that the mosquito population was unaffected by the rapture—proof positive that this place was going to hell in a handbasket.

We walked over to Priest's SUV where he and Garrett were talking. As we approached, they both glanced at me warily. I was definitely in the doghouse. I found it amusing that they were at odds with each other on so many things, including me, and yet they bonded so easily when I was on the outs with them.

"Plotting revenge on me?" I joked, hoping to lighten the mood. "Or is my surprise birthday party coming early this year?" It didn't work.

Garrett and Priest exchanged looks before Priest spoke. "How are you feeling?" I could tell there were more questions beyond that, but I was pretty sure he wasn't going to ask them until we were alone.

"Umm, good, I think." He perked his brow at *think*. "I guess I owe you both some apologies."

Priest glanced to Garrett, who promptly looked away from all of us. Why did I have a talent for stepping on everyone's hottest nerves?

"We can get into all that later," Priest changed the subject. I couldn't tell if he was being defensive of Garrett, or avoiding the topic out of irritation. "Right now I'd like you to tell me what you felt from that grim."

"I told you," I said, a little more snappish than I would have preferred. "It felt like I was looking into hell." A warm breeze feathered through my hair, defying its purpose by giving me goosebumps.

"How can that be?" Devin asked. "I thought you took the grim out of the glimmer. Shouldn't she have felt nothing?" Devin pulled out his cigarettes. He offered me one and I realized it had been forever since I had joined him in the disgusting habit. I took one just to see if Garrett or Priest would disapprove. They both watched me light it with interest, like they were discovering a whole new facet of my personality. I was now the rebellious, fearless Lenore, unconcerned for the future of my soft tissues.

I slipped the cigarette between my fingers and deftly puckered the first drags into the air to get it lit from Devin's proffered lighter. I drew back for my first full inhalation and coughed on it. Priest turned away biting back his smile. Yeah, I was still me—boring, coy, and health conscious.

"Yeah, why did I feel anything?" I asked after I had gotten a few shallow sips off my cigarette to prove it wasn't my first.

Priest crossed his arms and leaned against his vehicle. "I suspect that our crystalline dead are the path out of hell. The demons want to get into this world, but they need a host to do it. The Earth fully populated is a melting pot of sin, but it is also a melting pot of faith. When everyone was here, we balanced each other out. Now that all the... *true* believers are gone," Priest seemed to have trouble saying the words, even though he knew he was the exception, "everyone left behind is left is angry, confused, and bathing in whatever debauchery they damn well please. That means the Earth is now a petri dish to sustain them, and the crystalline dead are easy vessels to get them in."

"So even though there's no one on the line, the phone is still connected?" Devin simplified.

Priest nodded. I sighed, thinking about how many thousands of angry minds were on the other side of that grim portal. They all wanted in. They all wanted a chance to express their rage and mollify their pain with godless acts of pain and violence.

The only comforting thought was that with each passing day, more and more grim were becoming obsolete. The fewer bodies there were, the fewer demons there would be. At least, that was the running theory.

Something about the grim extermination still bothered me. It made sense to remove the puppets from the puppet masters, but something about it always gave me pause. Were we just trading in one problem for another? Would eliminating the grim leave the humans to fight each other? Were we better off with a focal point and purpose—idle hands and all?

"What is it?" Priest asked, seeing me trudging through my thoughts.

I glanced around as if he had put a spotlight on me and I still hadn't memorized my lines. "Oh... ah... nothing."

"Nothing?" He was reading me like a book. It might have been romantic for a man to know you well enough to read your thoughts off your face, but it was also damned annoying. Especially since the romance part was decidedly off limits, leaving me with a nosy friend.

I shook my head and shrugged, still trying to make him drop the subject. I was just running thoughts through my head. Until I had an actual theory, or something resembling a complete hypothesis, there was no point in prattling on. I didn't want to be the type of person who posed questions without having any answers to back it up.

"Lenore," Priest scolded. Damn, he was persistent. "You need to start sharing your intuition. Everyone is running without a leader right now. We can all hustle in a general direction, but you need to start leading like August wanted."

"What?" Devin asked, blowing out the last of his smoky breath before facing me.

"Shut up," I ground out to Priest.

Garrett looked between me and Priest. "What did August want?" he asked, mostly interested in anything August might have said.

"Before she died, August made Lenore promise—"

"Priest!"

Priest continued uninterrupted by my reprisal. "—to take her place and lead all of you."

"She said what?" Devin's voice was a whisper. I frowned before I even saw his puppy dog eyes staring back at me. I wasn't sure what he was more upset by: the fact that August had designated me as the leader instead of him, or that I hadn't been honest about it.

"Devin, she just... she was dying. I had to reassure her. I'm not going to take her place, she—"

Devin flicked his cigarette and walked a few steps away, not letting me finish. I wasn't sure what was worse—him being mad at me, or him being hurt by me. Luckily for me, I didn't have to choose. I had both.

"Why didn't you tell me this?" Garrett asked and I turned my apologetic gaping mouth to him. "You confided in *him*?" He motioned to Priest, who was smartly staying quiet, though a little late to earn any points with me. Now, because of him, I had a double-decker doghouse to stay the night in.

"No, I didn't confide in him. I opened my mouth and words fell out. He doesn't exactly let partial statements stand." I glared at Priest for effect, but Garrett moved in front of him, drawing my full attention back to him.

"How could you not tell me what my sister's last request was? Do you know how significant it was for her to bestow that duty on you with her last breath? She must have had tremendous faith in you if she gave you that honor, and not... anyone else?" His pause made me wonder if he hadn't hoped to lead our little band of misfits, but as he wasn't one to brag or boast he would never admit to thinking as much.

"Why do you think I didn't tell you?" I glanced over at Devin. He turned slightly, acknowledging that he was listening to my explanation even if he didn't want to. "You're all so committed to August and her quest. You wouldn't have thought twice about letting me lead if it was her wish. Even if it meant I wasn't ready. Even if I put everyone in danger."

"If she wanted you to lead, then you should lead," Devin snarled, but still refused to look me in the eye.

"Sometimes leading means stepping aside so someone else can do what needs to be done. We all have useful skills in this group. Each of us contributes. I'll admit I started out pretty much as a freeloader to this team, and just when I thought I earned the right to be a part of it, August died, leaving a new burden on my shoulders. Somewhere between grief, dishonor, and panic I decided I wasn't ready to stand up and take the reins. Foisting that responsibility on me isn't going to change that. I'm only starting to understand all this crap in my head and how to control it. I don't care what August said, and I don't care what everyone else thinks I'm capable of. I am telling you all right now: I am not ready!"

Garrett wanted to argue the point more, but he wisely nodded and got into the vehicle. Devin still held onto his scowl, but he finally looked at me. "I don't want to disappoint you again," I whispered loud enough to be heard over the chasm he was leaving between us. His eyes widened before looking down.

"You should have told me."

"I just told you why I didn't."

"You should have told *me*." He enunciated the words as if I didn't speak English well. There was so much emotion injected into his words I wasn't sure how to respond without hurting him.

"I thought you wanted to be the hero. Isn't that what you said?"

"No, I said I wanted to be *your* hero. You said I already was, remember?"

"You are."

"Then don't treat *me* like a sidekick." He stepped over to me, blocking my view of Priest who was patiently waiting to get into the Tahoe. "No more secrets, okay?"

I nodded and he kissed my forehead before ushering me to the vehicle.

Bad Timing

WHEN WE GOT BACK, Devin was in the front door before I even made it out of the vehicle. It occurred to me rather belatedly he was probably going to tell Haden about my untenured promotion. Somehow, dealing with her seemed more daunting than all three men. Haden was like a sister to me, but she was definitely an older, domineering, and slightly abusive sister. Being ranked under me in the title category wasn't going to sit well with her.

"Garrett," I called after him as he made it to the door ahead of me. I had yet to apologize for airing our relationship complications in the middle of my rage rant. I wasn't sure there was an appropriate apology for outing an adulterous relationship, but I would have to try.

Garrett looked back at me, waiting for a better lure than his name.

"Lenore, we need to talk," Priest said behind me. I looked back and saw that he looked as serious as he sounded. I resisted the "fuck off" I wanted to dole out, and brought my attention back to Garrett, who was already slipping in the door.

"Damn it, Priest." I didn't bother looking back at him before I stomped up the sidewalk to the house.

"We need to talk." I heard him following behind.

"Fuck off!" I didn't resist this time.

"Now!" He grabbed my arm in a harsh grip and pulled me to face him with his other hand. "I need answers and I don't—"

I twisted one arm out of his grip and punched him in the gut before clamping my hand on his throat. He recoiled at the jab, but didn't withdraw his grip on my other arm, nor did he try to remove my hand from his throat. "Do you have any idea what I could do to you right now?" I fumed, already planning out three different tactics that would leave him debilitated.

"Yes." He edged his free hand up to mine and clasped my wrist. "And you know what I can do," he whispered, not daring to make it sound like a threat so much as a reminder of previous evidence. I could feel the warmth in his fingertips threatening to come out.

As little as Priest knew about weapons and combat, he was fast becoming the biggest threat in our little band of warriors. Comparing my physical agility to his accord with God was like comparing pennies to diamonds.

I released my grip on his neck, letting my hand rest on his chest. He shifted, relaxing his stance and the grip on my arm and wrist, but he didn't let go. I hadn't been this close to him since the barn dance. It felt forever ago. The heat radiating off him was enough to remind me that anger wasn't the strongest emotion I felt for him. As mad as I was, my body was still responding to his proximity.

He must have felt the same way because his mouth went slack and his eyes danced over mine, dipping to look at my lips every time I licked them or bit them. He took in a deep breath, closed his eyes, and chanted something under his breath. A prayer or a blessing, I wasn't sure which. When he opened his eyes again, he looked pained.

"Lenore." His hand dropped and he took a long step back. The distance may as well have been a cold shower, as quickly as the hope of being with him drained away. "We need to talk about what you felt back there."

"We need to talk about what I felt right here."

Priest glanced back at the house as if he was afraid of getting caught being in a heated and lurid *discussion*. "I can't."

"You won't," I corrected, "and you've never told me why."

"Please, I can't explain. You won't understand."

"Try me. I have a right to know why the only man I've ever been in love with won't be with me." His eyes darted over mine, no doubt surprised at being my first love. I had obviously had other lovers, but I had never loved them. I loved Devin, but not in the way that compelled me to be near Priest. I cared for Garrett, but I couldn't define it as love.

"Lenore, you have to understand. Two years ago, I was completely devoted to God. My desires toward women were still a trial, but easily avoided with the right state of mind."

"Yes, and one year ago your orgasms were interspersed between bouts of inebriated highs. I think you can admit that neither lifestyle was a realistic approach to happiness."

Priest shifted his weight and crossed his arms. "Nevertheless, one is more appealing to me than the other."

"You can't possibly be serious. We've had this discussion already. You can't go back to being who you were!"

"Possibly not, but I would like the option left available to me."

"And being with me would prevent that?" I asked, only half serious.

"Yes." He raised his chin, challenging me to doubt him. "I want so much to be with you Lenore... in every way. But with you I would be lost. There would be no returning to the priesthood after that. Especially now, with these emerging powers, I think it's more important than ever that I not get distracted by a relationship with anyone other than Him."

I chuckled only because I didn't want him to know how deeply he had hurt me. I looked out onto the road and the vacant overgrown fields surrounding us. It should have been peaceful and serene, but something about this place made my skin crawl. I wanted to go back to the old house, but I couldn't bring myself to disappoint everyone.

"Aren't you going to say something?" Priest asked when I was quiet too long.

"What do you want me to say? I think your hope of remaining a priest post-apocalypse is like trying to ride a horse after you've shot it." Despite the ire of my tone, he smirked at the comment. "I think you're still an addict," I said, sobering his amusement. "As a priest you were pious, celibate, and constant in your faith. When your obsession in faith died with the rest of the world, you turned to sex and drugs."

Priest perked his brow at my interpretation, so I went on. "After you sobered up, you needed to find your fix somewhere else. I think you were hoping I could feed your addiction, but clearly that didn't work out. Now with this new power at your fingertips, you can move on to bigger and better thrills. I'm sure you thought you loved me—like an alcoholic might think they enjoy non-alcoholic beer, until they don't get their buzz." He shook his head at me, denying the claim. "Just be honest, Priest, so we can put this behind us, once and for all."

Priest set his jaw. "I've always been honest with you." His eyes fluttered over mine. "I do love you." He stepped toward me with predatory intent. I tensed for the attack, but I knew that wasn't the type of attack he had planned. His hand reached around my back, pulling me against him. His lips descended, but before our lips could touch, I heard glass breaking inside and Haden yelling.

Cat Fight

WE BOTH SNAPPED OUT of the romantic prelude and looked toward the house. I didn't bother making excuses to Priest. I twisted out of his embrace and ran to the rescue. I pushed inside the front door prepared to fight a gaggle of grim. Garrett was in the living room watching the skirmish with crossed arms. Haden was in the kitchen throwing dishes at Devin. He nonchalantly caught the ones he could and batted away or ducked the ones he couldn't.

Priest came in behind me, bumping into my back. "What's going on?" he asked, gently ushering me in so he could shut the door behind us.

"We are having a disagreement," Devin answered him sardonically.

"Clearly," I said. "Care to elaborate?"

"How could you not tell us?" Haden turned her threat of glassware bombs at me. I ducked out of the path of a bowl, which Priest safely caught and tossed to Devin so he could place it with the rest of the unbroken items on the island. "She wanted *you*!"

I glowered at Priest and shook my head. He didn't understand the delicate balance that was Haden. She was as tough as nails, but her grand ego was so easily shaken. "Haden, I didn't want to change our dynamic. Besides, we are a team. We don't need a leader."

"Yes, we do," Garrett insisted.

"Not helping, Garrett." I glared back at him, leaving myself open for a teacup that I barely ducked. "Haden stop, this doesn't change anything."

"I can't believe she chose you," Haden mumbled, searching for another item to throw.

It was easy enough to assume Haden had hoped to succeed August, but that wasn't what was bringing her to Greek-wedding antics. She could have submitted to August's choice of leader if it had been someone she respected and trusted.

I had a tenuous friendship with Haden. She accepted me as a member of the group, but only the way a family accepts their idiot cousin. It wasn't just her ego that disliked me being in charge. It was her sense of survival. To her, I was still the third sidekick.

To some extent, I hadn't fully let go of that title either, but if I was to remain in good standing with Haden, I only had one choice: I needed to prove I was worthy of August's high expectations. With Haden, there was only one way to do that.

Haden grabbed a saucer and spun it like a Frisbee at my head. I caught it and whipped it back at her hard. She didn't quite make it out of the way and the saucer skimmed her right temple and smashed into the cupboard behind her.

Haden's shock only lasted a moment. The rage returned and she jumped the railing separating the kitchen and living room to get at me. A slew of objections were bellowed at both of us, but I ignored everyone. I didn't care if I won or lost, but Haden was damn well going to know I could keep up with her.

I elbowed Priest to force him back, and ducked under Haden's attack, flipping her over my shoulder. I moved to get clear of her supine body, but she tripped me. I careened into the dining room table just short of earning a concussion.

She scrambled toward me, but I elbowed her in the head before she could get on top of me. I yanked my wrist from her persistent grip and we both jumped back up. Garrett moved around us, not attempting to stop the fight. He joined Priest and Devin who seemed to be debating when or whether to intervene.

Haden got close enough to grab and pull my hair. I pushed toward her tugging hand and head-butted her. While she was still dazed, I punched her in the stomach. She doubled over, but barreled into me, pushing me against the wall.

I hammered my fist down against her lower back. She moved away to gather herself and I moved away hoping she would call it good. Unfortunately, the anger in her eyes told me she wasn't going to let this go until she either won or needed first aid.

She crouched down and pulled out her hunting knife from her leg holster. A cacophony of new fervent objections sounded, but she threw the knife anyway. It was off by about a half foot, but I imagined she wanted it to land beside me in the drywall to prove she could hit me if she wanted to.

I didn't think much about it, but my hand flew up, catching the hilt of the knife as it passed. I tossed it right back at her. It dug into the back of the couch inches from what would have been disastrous to her internal organs.

Everyone seemed shocked that I was capable of the move. I had surprised myself as well, but I held my stoic unfazed expression.

Haden looked down at the knife sticking out of the upholstered frame, before turning her fiery eyes on me. I stared right back at her, refusing to cower in the face of her temper. I was done apologizing and I was done making excuses.

Nothing and everything changed in that moment. She was still a loud-mouthed, violent egomaniac, but I was no longer the third sidekick in her eyes. I may not have been worthy of the alpha-dog spot August had given me, but I had at least earned the right to get out of the stables.

Haden pulled her knife free and sheathed it. Without so much as a word, she headed back to her room. The men said nothing to either one of us. They seemed to understand what had transpired. I grabbed a broom and started sweeping. Sidekick or not, someone had to clean up this mess.

In the Still of the Night

MY STAY ON WATCH was as boring as ever. The cool air wasn't enough to show my breath, but it was enough to warrant a few extra jogs around the house to check for glimmer grim. I had my bow and arrow and was ready to use it, but unfortunately our new hideout was vastly less exciting than our old one.

Everyone was thrilled to have easy nights on the lookout, but I was still concerned there was a reason for the lack of activity. Bottom line was, if the grim weren't coming to get us, something was stopping them. What kept grim from coming to this house?

"What are you thinking about so hard?" Devin asked, interrupting my thoughts and boredom as he slipped out the patio doors.

"What are you doing up? I can go all night."

"I bet you can," he said seductively, followed by a yawn.

"I'm not sure you can, though." I chuckled and shifted to face him on the wooden rail I was straddling.

"Haden won't let me sleep," he said, leaning over the rail to enjoy the view, mostly of the trees, but occasionally of me.

"TMI," I grimaced.

"No—well yes, but she's pretty talkative tonight. She has a lot of concerns about…"

"Me?"

"The whole world. I think it's just now occurring to her that we might be battling something beyond the scope of her weaponry. All this *magic* is throwing her for a loop."

"Me and her both," I mumbled. "This afternoon was bad. I mean, really bad. I know people always talk about going to hell, but I never thought of it like that. It gets in your head. I was staring in the window for a few seconds and I wanted to kill Priest. It's no wonder the grim are a broken record of carnage."

"What were you thinking about so hard when I interrupted?"

I sucked in a breath and considered sloughing off the question, but I knew he wouldn't appreciate that, given our conversation earlier. "Priest said the demons need a host. A body to use as a portal out of hell." He nodded. "Do you think they could potentially use us as a portal? Living people?"

"I haven't kept up with my religion lessons, but isn't that what demons do? Possess people? I assume it's a lot easier getting into a hollow mind than an active one, though," Devin said, jumping right on the caboose of my train of thought.

"Right. So if a demon were to take over a human, they would have to be very strong." Devin nodded. "What if the reason I'm getting such an evil vibe off Adrian Dorn is because he's a puppet for a pretty powerful demon?"

Devin wasn't any more prepared to hear that than I was to say it. He rubbed his face and shook his head. "I don't care if he's the bogeyman, I'm not going to let that bastard get away with killing August, and he sure as hell isn't getting his hands on you."

I smiled and squeezed his shoulder. He was falling back into protection mode, but it wasn't me he was protecting. We were all under the impression the battle we would be fighting was going to involve guns and knives. Now, like Haden, we were figuring out this whole "magic" thing was going to be more important than we thought.

House Guests

A FTER DEVIN HEADED BACK to bed, I continued my boring watch. On my thirtieth run around the house, I returned to the backyard to find a grim ambling up the incline toward the house. I loaded my arrow and shot him. When he went down, I almost cheered. It was nice to finally have something to do.

I pulled my machete from my belt and sauntered over to finish the job. The grim squirmed face down like a fish out of water. I raised the blade and slammed it into his neck. It crunched through the tissue like papier-mâché and stuck until I pulled it back.

I stood looking over the stilled creature carefully. It hadn't shattered the way a grim usually did. Even in the full moon's light, the skin looked dull gray, without a hint of the sandy glimmer that earned them their name.

I kept my machete in hand while I pushed the creature over on its back. It flopped over, leaving the head behind. The creature was wearing a suit and tie, more formal than the usual grim. The shriveled skin on the hands made for boney fingers.

This was not a grim.

I cursed quietly and knelt down to flip the head. I rolled it over confirming my suspicions. The sunken cheeks and eyes were paired with attenuated lips. This was a corpse.

The eyes cracked open and I jumped back. The body attempted to move but seemed unable to get purchase. I shot it with another arrow in the head, but the desiccated body didn't seem to rely on that body part to function.

I stood up prepared to fetch Devin for a consult on the strange development. I was met with a line of a dozen gray corpses that had appeared at the base of the lawn inside the tree line. I backed away, scanning the shadows for more, but I wasn't surrounded. I leaped onto the deck and ripped open the patio door. "Devin!" I yelled as loudly and urgently as I could.

While I waited, the corpses waddled themselves up the hill, still in formation. Garrett jumped outside first, prepared to fight. He glanced over the line, not understanding what they were. I put my arm out before he could leap over the rail and start uselessly pummeling them.

"What the fuck?" Devin came out shirtless with his pajama bottoms on. Haden stumbled out behind him in his pajama top with a gun in hand. Before I could stop her, she fired shots along the line. The bodies faltered from the blast, but the bullets went through them without any hint of damage.

"Why aren't they shattering?" Haden asked, loading another round.

"They aren't grim. Stop shooting."

"What are they?" Devin asked.

"They're corpses. Real corpses," I said, still searching my mind for an answer to a question I hadn't even developed yet.

"You've got to be kidding me," Haden objected. "Night of the living dead? Like grim weren't enough." Despite my moratorium on bullets, she tried a couple more shots with the same non-results.

"We need Priest," I blurted out, successfully finding something that resembled a plan in my brain. I whipped around to fetch him.

"He's not here," Garrett said, reaching across to stop me from going in.

"What?" I glanced at Devin, but he didn't seem to know anything about it either. "Where did he go? It's the middle of the night."

"I'm not his keeper," Garrett said.

"Then why are you the only one who knows he left?" I snarled.

"*Fallen.*" A hoarse whisper reached me, so close to my ear that I ducked forward and swung around fists first to defend myself. There was no one behind me.

"Did you hear that?" I asked. The blank stares I received answered my question. I ignored the dubious gazes that suggested I was off my rocker. If they hadn't figured out by now I was special in the head, they weren't paying attention.

I forgot about my argument and stepped back to the railing. The pre-apocalyptic dead stared back at me, each with their own version of eyes. One in particular had a glass eye. I focused on it, simply because it looked less icky than the blackened depressions on the others.

"Are you speaking to me?" I asked, hoping and dreading the answer. If they answered, I wasn't crazy, but if they did, then—holy shit they're talking to me.

"*Trespasser,*" was the only response given. The word sounded so close I had to resist the urge to swat it away from my ear like a buzzing fly.

"Who are you? What are you?"

"*We are the first. We are the eldest.*" The voice was mechanical in delivery, but authoritative.

"Lenore, what are you doing?" Garrett grabbed me as I gravitated off the deck to get closer to them.

"I can hear them." I shrugged him away, but he followed me down, preparing his gun on the way. "Are you demons?" I asked.

"*We are the first. We are the eldest. We are the Seraphim.*"

"I suppose that would mean something to me if I had a priest to explain it to me," I grumbled to myself. "Why are you here?" I asked louder.

"*Our land... trespasser. We are the first to claim. The Earth is forfeit.*"

"Like hell it is. The Earth belongs to the human race. We may be a little underpopulated, but we aren't going anywhere." Since the line hadn't moved closer, I continued to move toward them.

"*Humans are forfeit. Humans are fodder for demons.*"

I shook my head even though I knew arguing with a telepathic corpse was pointless. "You're wrong. We'll fight. We'll survive." I stopped in front of my glassy-eyed foe.

"*No survival.*" The voice was firmer, but the volume was still the same. "*Only clemency or oblivion.*"

As stupid as it was, I reached out and touched the corpse with the glass eye. Garrett yelled at me, but his voice was gone as soon as I touched it. A face gauzy and brilliant towered over and behind the carcass. A pair of large wings jutted from his back, four tiny wings adorned his face—two in place of eyebrows, and two as laurel leaves crowning his head.

"*Submit.*" I felt the power that filled his words with authority. His demand vibrated through my body and dropped me to my knees. I could no more deny him my deference, than a dog could deny his owner obedience. I was nothing to this being.

Before I realized it, Garrett was dragging me away, severing the connection. Another round of bullets penetrated our walking dead guests, but they were nothing more than marionettes to the beings holding them, a scare tactic at best. Nevertheless, the corpses turned and disappeared back into the trees.

Once Before a Time

"**W**HY DO WE HAVE to leave?" Haden objected as I packed up our food. Garret and Devin were already packing up, but she wasn't as easy to convince.

"Because, Haden, the Earth is forfeit and if these creatures want this land, I assure you there isn't going to be an argument from us."

"Why the hell not? They didn't even attack us."

"They didn't need to."

Haden objected further, putting her hand in the way of my box. "We have a right to be here."

"No, Haden, we don't," I said somberly. "I don't know what those things are, but they aren't those corpses. They just used them to scare us away. Look." I touched her hand gently to appeal to her, but she dragged it away, freeing me to continue packing. "These aren't demons we are dealing with, but they are clearly not to be messed with. Whoever or whatever Seraphim are, they are powerful."

"Seraphim?" Priest asked from the front door. He was just getting home.

I glanced over his dirt-laden clothes and checked the clock. It was after three a.m. He had left before my watch, and was now arriving after my watch. "Where the hell have you been?"

He kicked off his mud-caked boots. "Minor projects, don't worry about it. What's this about Seraphim?"

"We are being kicked out by them." Haden stopped fighting my packing and started helping. That of course meant slamming every can as loudly as possible to make sure her objections still stood.

"What are they?" I asked Priest, since he seemed to know the name.

"They are in the first hierarchy of angels, believed to have inhabited the earth long before God created man." My mouth went slack and Haden stopped smacking her cans.

"I didn't think there was anything before man," I said.

"We're being kicked out by angels?" Haden shrieked. "I thought angels were the good guys."

Priest shrugged. "Good guys, yes, but not necessarily on the same team." Haden scoffed and stormed out of the room yelling our new discovery to Devin. "What happened?" Priest approached me slowly.

"Some clumsy corpses—real corpses—came right up to our backyard. I could hear their thoughts. When I touched one I could see the Seraphim behind it." I took in a deep breath and let it out slowly. "Priest, what is all of this? They said the Earth is forfeit. They said we are fodder for demons. That's not true, is it? He didn't leave us here as a sacrifice to make nice with His enemies, did He?"

Priest shook his head, but it wasn't to negate my statement. "There are so many stories, Lenore. I can't tell you anything for certain, but I do know this: Each one of us still has a chance to make it back to God. We just have to earn it."

"How do you know that?" I stepped forward and pulled a twig of some kind from his hair.

"I just do." He backed away from me. "I'm going to go clean up if there's time." I nodded and he left me to my packing.

Home Squatted Home

The old house was still abandoned. Haden was sick about returning to it, but Devin headed up to his old room without complaint. Priest headed upstairs after Garrett, while I started a fire to take the chill out of the house.

The sun was pinking the sky so there was no need for anyone to be on watch, but I found myself reluctant to go upstairs. Part of it was because I didn't want to deal with fending off Garrett's advances, which were becoming more needy than loving. The other reason I stayed downstairs was to think.

The apocalypse left very little room for assumptions about the existence of God. When the silver saints were mobilized by demons, it put hell back on the map for a lot of non-believers as well. I had long suspected Adrian Dorn was being controlled by an uber demon—who apparently had a crush on me—and now uber angels were staking claim to the Earth like it was the Oklahoma territory.

Aside from the obvious question of, "*Why here?*" I still had a slew of questions that needed answers. I wasn't sure Priest was going to have them. He was well-read in biblical history, but as he said, there were so many stories. How could we distinguish between varying religious beliefs, let alone the subjective watered-down history within them all?

There wasn't exactly a guide for dealing with post-apocalyptic entities at the local library.

"What are you thinking about so hard?" Garrett asked coming down the stairs.

So much for avoiding him.

"Everything." I shrugged.

"Come to bed." He smiled warmly. It was hard to say no when he made the effort to be sweet.

Perhaps it was the realization that there were even more strange things going on in the world, or the fact that everyone was expecting me to lead them to some great victory over the grim, but I decided to finally man up and say what had been on my mind for weeks. "Don't you miss your wife?"

The question shattered his smile and he scanned the stairwell as if he were embarrassed to discuss it with me. "Yeah, sure," he said, joining me on the couch. I shifted to face him, and prevent him from getting his hands around me.

"You said you had priorities in Chicago, but you haven't been back to see her in months."

"Don't worry about it," he said, touching my leg.

"What changed?" I asked.

"I think that question should be directed at you," he said.

"You know what changed for me. You told me you were married and more so that you still love her. That kind of admission tends to put a damper on one's libido."

"I told you. I can't be with her."

"You're running, Garrett. You're running away from the pain."

"It's what we both want."

"Are you sure about that? She looked pretty happy to see you at the last tournament. She missed you."

"Why are we even talking about this?" he grumbled.

"Because we never did talk about it."

"Yes, we did," he argued.

"Garrett, I don't want to be caught between you and her."

"You aren't. She is there. You are here. Never the twain shall meet. Get it?"

"Yeah, that's the part that doesn't work for me."

"Is this about commitment? Do you want something more, because I can't leave my wife? Not now, not after everything we've been through. That's too cruel."

"No, Garrett, I'm not asking you to leave your wife. I'm asking you to go back to her."

"Don't be ridiculous. We still have work to do."

I chuckled. "You'll notice your objection to leaving here has nothing to do with me."

"Lenore, don't do this. We are great together."

"In bed we are great together. In battle we are great together. In reality, I'm just here."

His eyes widened slightly and he shook his head. "I'm not going to leave you to fight alone."

"I'm not asking you to. I'm just asking you to go back to Chicago. We'll see you at the tournaments. We can go from there, okay?"

Garrett suddenly stood up and looked around the room as if it was to blame for my sudden change of character. "You want me to leave right now?"

"No, of course not," I chided. "Get some rest."

Garrett glanced at the stairs and back at me. "Come up with me, please."

I shook my head. "Garrett, I'm not going to change my mind about this. I'm sorry you're hurting. I'll do what I can to help you through this, but I can't be your retreat from reality anymore. There is a woman in Chicago who is feeling the same pain you are. Go to her. Comfort each other."

He wavered, perhaps hoping to change my mind, but when it was clear I had made a firm decision, he disappeared upstairs.

It wasn't long before he came back down with his coat on and bag in hand. I tipped my head at him, disappointed he was going to storm out. He paused by the front/back door, looking me over. "What if I can't bear to be with her? What if it's too much?"

"Then leave her... for good. Either way, one of us is going to lose you, and she was here first. She should at least get first dibs."

He nodded. I was tempted to go to him and kiss him goodbye, but the little part of me that feared being alone might never want to let him go. He seemed to be debating the same thing. He came to the same conclusion and walked out. A moment later his motorcycle roared to life and sped off.

Answers

"I DON'T THINK SO." Devin stood firmly between me and the kitchen door with his arms crossed.

The argument had been going on for nearly an hour. It was three to one with me on the losing side. Apparently, being the chosen leader held no weight when you were volunteering yourself for a suicide mission.

"Lenore, you may not be ready for this." Priest stood by the table with reticent concern on his face.

"Ready or not, what the hell is the point?" Haden quibbled by the stove. "Shit's going to go down eventually, who cares what the background story is? Just cap the bad guys and move on."

I shook my head. "I just need to understand what is going on. What are we dealing with here?"

"You know what we're dealing with," Devin said. "You saw it when you touched that grim and considering your reaction then, I don't want you going near an *old* one."

"I'm not going to read it. I'm going to talk to it."

"Your mind will still be at risk," Devin scolded.

"I only need a few minutes," I petitioned.

"No!" Devin yelled, making me jump. "I'm not losing any more of this team. You aren't going and that's the end of it." I tipped my chin up obstinately. "Lenore, I will tie you up if you don't promise me not to do this."

"I won't be able to keep that promise if I make it," I said apologetically. Devin grabbed me and threw me over his shoulder. I didn't bother fighting since I knew he could subdue me even on my best days. "Devin stop it! I need to do this!"

"And I need you to stay put." He took me into the living room and tossed me on the couch, after which he sat on me.

"Hey!" I yelped.

"This should do it. What's rerunning on the broadcast, Haden?" Devin smiled at Haden and she smiled back. Glad to see they found something to bond over.

"Priest!" I struggled to see him around Devin's head. He was still in the kitchen contemplating something. "You know I'm right, don't you?" He turned to look at me. The concern on his face was growing.

"He doesn't know anything." Devin shifted, putting a little more pressure on me, though I knew it wasn't his full weight.

"I'm going to pee on you," I threatened.

"Not really my style, baby, but whatever turns you on." There was a consensus "eww" from Haden and me.

"I think we should let her go," Priest said, finally joining us in the living room. Both Haden and Devin shot eye daggers at him. "If you want her to guide us, she has to have the answers to her questions. Instincts are helpful in the moment, but we can't predict anything accurately without knowledge."

"Exactly," I agreed.

"Interviewing a grim is not going to get her answers. It's going to get her soul eaten," Devin fumed.

Priest looked me over. "Her soul is tethered pretty tight. I think she'll be alright, but I want to go with her." I opened my mouth to object, but Devin clamped his hand over it. Despite my muffled objections, and my hands wrenching at his wrist, the conversation went on without me.

"You think you can knock out a demon as easily on an old grim?" Devin asked.

"Maybe not as easily, but they seem to be loosely connected no matter what age they are. At worst, I'll just have to work a little harder."

Devin looked at me and I silenced my stifled profanities. The thumb of his smothering hand caressed my cheek. He turned back to Priest. "You understand what is at stake here?"

"I won't let anything happen to her," he answered.

"Good, because if you do…" Devin smiled, letting the sentence trail off for Priest's imagination to finish. He unclasped my mouth and shifted his weight off me to sit beside me. "What about you?" He poked my nose, and I batted his hand away. "Do you understand what is at stake here?" He poked my ribs, making me squirm.

"No, that's why I want to go see the grim." I glared.

He grabbed my hand and pressed it flat to his chest. "Do you know what is at stake here?" he whispered. I frowned and nodded. He kissed my hand before getting up. "Okay. If you must do this, then we all go." He looked to Haden and she nodded in agreement. "Haden and I will wait outside in case there is trouble. You and Priest can go inside to interview the grim. That is assuming the crazy old coot lets you in."

Knock Knock

T HE ONLY HOUSE TO survive our cleansing efforts was the smallest of the group. The boarded-up windows were a marker of the apocalyptic recluse, the ones who hoarded food and supplies with the expectation of living out their days holed up in their homes.

I had to admit, the idea had crossed my mind when I first heard about the grim. My desire to run from danger made the prospect reasonable, but in the end, it was still my fear of loneliness and my claustrophobia that kept me from becoming a hermit.

As I stood before the house, I wondered if I was ready for what was inside. Everyone had the potential to go off the deep end. It took ten days to decide on suicide, but what about the thirty-day mark? What about the year mark?

When did the crazy set in so deep, you couldn't get it out again?

That was what the new world was: the crazies and the walking dead—and I don't mean the grim.

"You okay?" Priest asked next me. I drew my gaze from the house and gave him a fake smile. "Don't do that. Don't pretend with me."

I lost my smile and went back to staring at the door. "I'm scared of what's inside," I answered honestly.

"That's why I'm here."

"I'm not afraid of the grim. I just know that house is thick with crazy, and I don't want any to sink in." I looked back at him. "You know we're all just teetering on the brink of insanity, right?"

Priest nodded, though I think he would have argued that he'd been there, done that. "Come on. I won't let the crazy sink in either." He gave my shoulder a squeeze.

We started walking toward the house, and to my surprise he took my hand in his. I glanced at the comforting gesture and wondered if he would have still done it if Garrett was around. I hadn't told everyone the details of our breakup. I only told them he had gone back to Chicago until the next tournament.

It was the truth. There was still a chance he could choose me. Part of me didn't want him to, but only the part that still hoped Priest would give up his ridiculous fantasy of being solely devoted to God again. The part that wanted Garrett to choose me was the scared, lonely, attention starved girl I tried not to listen to, but inevitably gave in to far too often.

"Thank you," I said as we reached the door, "for supporting me on this."

Priest looked like he wanted to say something, but he let it pass and turned to the door. After a pause he knocked loudly. I could hear the faint sound of music from inside before a door slammed. Footsteps came toward us, stopping behind the door. We waited for a response, but the homeowner said nothing.

I heard the mail slot open, and I shoved Priest to one side just in time to save him from knee-shattering shotgun pellets. I dove down in the opposite direction. As soon as I landed, I bounced back up and plastered myself to house. Priest did the same.

"Get the hell off my property!" a man yelled from behind the door.

"We aren't here to steal from you!" I yelled back. "We aren't here to harm you in any way."

"What do you want?" he shouted.

"I want to talk to your... wife." I hoped I had discerned the relation correctly. There was a long pause. Priest and I exchanged a weary look. I was reasonably certain the man wouldn't continue to waste shells, but there was no telling what his state of mind was. "The woman upstairs. I need to speak to her. It's very important."

"Why?" he asked.

"She may have..." I blanked on a logical explanation that didn't involve questioning a demon. I looked to Priest for some kind of cover story that this lunatic might buy into enough to let us inside.

"She's been chosen by God," Priest said. My eyes bugged out with concern that he had just added religious psychobabble to an already struggling mind. He shrugged at me as if to say, *you asked.*

"She has?" the man asked with interest.

"Yes," I continued. "There are so few good people left on the Earth. It's our job to find them and learn from them. Please, we only wish to speak to her. Then we'll go and never bother you again."

There was another long pause.

The barrel slid back and the mail slot clanked shut. There were a several creaks inside. It sounded like he was pulling nails out of the boards securing the door. I looked at Priest, still fearful of the crazy we were about to enter into. He moved across the entrance and stood next to me. After a moment, he grabbed my hand again. It was such a small thing, holding hands, but it made me feel so much stronger.

When the door finally squawked open, the shotgun poked out first, and I had to resist the urge to grab the muzzle and kick the door in. That probably would have been the wisest move, but so far this man hadn't done anything wrong.

At least not to us.

When the man emerged from behind the door, his stench made me turn away to gather my composure. He smelled of body odor and a melee of other things: food, smoke, Old Spice cologne and alcohol.

His hair was a ragged grayish brown with a beard to match. His skin was deathly pale from being inside too long. He squinted at the afternoon light that was painful to his eyes. His wrinkled flannel pajamas looked like they had sat in the dryer too long. In addition to his shotgun, he had a tool belt that doubled as a knife holster and shell holder.

He looked over the two of us warily, and I did my best to appear nonthreatening. Priest made sure to pull out the cross necklace I had made him so the man would see we were God-fearing people. Or at least one of us was. Fear didn't quite sum up my opinion of God.

"Come, come." The man ushered us in frantically. He must have presumed we were in danger of being attacked by looters at any moment. Little did he know the only people stupid enough to try to get into this house, was us. That point drove home harder when the hermit shut the door and started hammering the boards back against it.

How the Other Half Live

I SQUEEZED PRIEST'S HAND, which he had thankfully not taken away from me yet. My bravery failed me at the strangest times. My claustrophobia flared in the humid, dimly lit home. He clasped my hand just as tightly. I felt his warmth flood into me like a contrast shot, settling my nerves.

Once I had calmed, I took in my surroundings. There wasn't a foyer, except what was designated by floor tiles. The living room took the length of the house, minus the study, which held boxes floor to ceiling. There was a staircase off to the right leading to the second floor. Past the stairs, at the rear of the house, I determined to be the kitchen and dining room, each of which exuded their own set of smells.

The music I had heard was coming from behind the dining room door. It was classical. Nothing mournful like the house deserved, but rather upbeat and dramatic. It must have been a soundtrack to an opera or a ballet. Looking around the living room, I could see piles of books.

The far corner contained a section devoted to an easel and canvas. The painting had only begun to form, but I could already make out the features of a woman's face. "What's her name?" I asked without thinking what emotion I might extrude.

The man turned his attention from the door and shoved his hammer into his belt. I was pleased that he was content with only one board. Perhaps we could pay homage to classic horror movies with a narrow escape. Assuming we could get the hammer from the psychopath.

Why the hell was I here again?

"Avery," he said, following my gaze to the painting. He looked forlorn for a moment, but it passed when he spoke. "Do you think she's really been chosen by God?"

"Yes," Priest said before I could answer. "It was a mistake that she was left."

The man smiled, showing off his lack of dental care. "I'll show you to her room. You can't stay long, though. She gets restless with new people." He moved past us and led the way upstairs.

The windows on the upper level were uncovered, offering a respite from the bleak darkness downstairs. I caught a glimpse into the bedrooms as I passed. I gasped when I saw a set of twin beds in the first room, complete with two young crystalline boys.

Carefully placed under the covers, they each held matching teddy bears in their arms. They weren't animated yet, as with most of the young crystalline dead. It was the only functioning miracle left on earth.

In the next room was a nursery. I presumed within the plush crib was a crystalline baby, but I didn't attempt to confirm my suspicions. I just tucked in a little closer to Priest, who offered yet another dose of warmth into my body.

As we approached the far room, formerly the master bedroom, a yowl stopped my feet. It was mournful like a woman, and angry like an animal. "Don't be shy," the husband said, trying to grab my arm. I pulled away with a smile and moved forward again.

At the door, the husband unlocked it and pushed it open forcefully as if something was behind it. The room was bright with stark white furniture. The walls were a creamy brown with gold-framed pictures that made it look like a high-class hotel rather than a bedroom.

The woman on the bed didn't resemble the painting except for the color of her auburn hair. Her face was sallow and her body starved. Since the crystalline dead kept their original physique, I assumed the woman was an anorexic in her living life.

Her hair was cut shorter than the painting, and I could see bald patches. The demon must have taken to ripping at the hair.

She looked us over curiously as we entered, but remained quiet. Being so close to a glassy-eyed grim made every instinct in my body scream at me to run. It was my very favorite response to danger, but in this case, running would cause more trouble than it was worth.

Priest pulled away from my hand, and I felt naked. He moved casually to the window as if to enjoy the view, but I knew he was showing himself to Haden and Devin so they knew we were inside and safe. So far.

"My precious, you have visitors. Don't you want to say hello?" The husband asked, daring to sit right next to her on the bed. She hissed at his presence, baring her teeth, but the restraints holding her to the bed kept her from doing more.

I tried to find some comfort in the fact that this grim was an evil demon and not the man's real wife, but somehow I still felt sympathy for the strange circumstances. There had to be some room to pity the enemy, or you couldn't claim to be the good guys.

Priest stayed by the window, leaving me at the foot of the four-poster bed to stare into predatory eyes. The husband still held his shotgun, and I knew I couldn't ask the questions I wanted to with him present. The offense he would take might cost me my life.

"Could we speak to her alone?" I asked gingerly.

The man looked as hurt as he did offended. I resisted the urge to offer a reason for the request. I wanted to appear stoic and mysterious to him, like any good religious guru should. He looked to Avery as if asking permission. She never took her eyes off me, but a new smile blossomed on her face.

She was looking forward to this conversation.

Bread Crumbs

A VERY'S EYES FOLLOWED ME as I moved around the room. She was sizing me up, trying to figure out my game so she could plan hers. The last time I was in the presence of an animated grim with the capability of speech, it could read my thoughts like a book. Lucky for me, I had no idea what I was doing. That would at least keep her guessing, since I would be guessing as well.

I glanced at Priest, which was probably a mistake. Her eyes darted to him. She was already figuring out he was more of a threat to her than I was—if she even considered me a threat. Priest didn't respond to her glare, he just watched patiently, staying close to the window so Haden and Devin didn't try to break down the door prematurely.

I moved around the bed to get closer to her. I noticed the various bottles of moisturizer and perfumes sitting on the dresser adjacent to the bed. Her husband was very confused about the difference between dry skin and *desiccated* skin.

The trash bin unfortunately caught my eye as well. A used condom hung off the edge of the wicker basket. I winced, trying not to think of the necrophilia this man was partaking in. Some part of me was not surprised, but another part of me was keeping a strangled hold on my gag reflex.

"Tick tock." Avery spoke, tipping her head with the tick and tock. I assumed she was getting tired of waiting for me to initiate the dialogue.

"I've come to ask you some questions," I said.

"Get on with it, skin." Her voice was normal, which still didn't make sense to me since her vocal chords should have solidified. I always expected the demon to speak through them, like the Seraphim had.

"Can you read my thoughts?" I asked.

"Just the loud ones." She winked at me.

"You're a demon, right?" It was a pubescent level to start at, but I didn't want to make any assumptions, considering we now had angels running around in our graveyards.

"I suppose that is what *you* would call me."

I took that as an insult to my intelligence, but since I didn't want to get confused on the subtle variations of demons, I continued. "What do you want?"

She perked an eyebrow. "I want you and all your kind to hurt the way I do. I want your blood spilled. I want to watch the pain in your eyes as you die." Since I was familiar with the realm this creature came from, the unjustified bloodlust was not surprising to me.

"You want to eat our souls."

"I only need your agony. I have my own soul." That part did surprise me.

"Demons don't have souls," Priest said from the window.

"Then you should choose me another name." Avery locked eyes with him and licked her lips—as best she could. "You have fallen hard from grace. It's easy to lose your bearings in the service of one so taciturn." Priest managed not to react to her bait, but I could see him clenching his fists.

"What are you, if not a demon?" I asked.

"Come closer and see the truth for yourself," she drawled.

I stepped forward and Priest jumped to attention. "Lenore."

"What do you think I came here for, Priest?" I said without ceremony.

"You said you wouldn't read her. You're not ready," he whispered despite the demon—or whatever—hearing us both clearly.

"How will I get ready?" I looked to him, hoping he had an answer to that question, but he resigned himself to coming closer to the bed, in case he needed to pull me away.

I sat down next to the grim. I reached to touch her face and she snapped her teeth at my fingers. She laughed uproariously, satisfied that she had startled me.

I forced my curiosity in front of my fear and pressed my hand to her chest over her sternum. I expected an immediate reaction, but my mind lingered on details: the strangeness of a mobile body without a heartbeat or warmth, the feel of her skin—gritty, yet pliable enough to bend and flex—the smell of something burning.

My mind slipped away from the reality I was already uncomfortable with and dropped into a mirror image. Everything I saw was the same, but in the negative, white to black, light to dark. Priest was gone, and the grim before me was a faceless black body surrounded by cool, painless flames.

I looked in the mirror to see if I had changed, but all I saw was the reflection of the world I had just left. I could see Priest watching me intently. He looked torn between letting me do what I needed to do and trying to save me.

"What do you seek, child of God?" The black mass spoke, but nothing resembling a mouth offered the words. The voice was finally what I anticipated: gravelly and hoarse.

"I seek the truth," I said.

"I have only my truth. I have only my sins to hold me for eternity and my rage to burn me while I wait. What more truth do you seek?"

"You said you have a soul."

"Yes, but it is lost. Lost, lost, lost…"

"These bodies, the grim, can a real demon possess them? Could they use them to get on earth?"

"Demons have always been on earth. They are parasites, but they need vessels to walk among us."

"Can they possess living people? Are there demons possessing people now?"

The black shape seemed to shrug as if it didn't know, or wouldn't say. "The great demons hold us back. Hold us in this hell. We feed it with our anger and envy, but it's not enough. It is so hungry. We will never be enough. Nothing will ever be enough. It will always be hungry."

"Can these demons feed off our souls?"

"Yes, as many as your God has left for them."

I tried not to think about that added insult on top of being deserted. "Why would he leave us here to feed demons if it won't slake their hunger?"

The black mass shook with laughter. "He didn't leave you as bread to feed them. He left you because you are crumbs. The bread has already been taken."

I drew back my hand as the blob started to laugh again. The world faded around me and when I reawakened in the original version of the room, Priest was holding my free hand. "Are you okay?" he asked, crouched below me by the bed with one hand on the grim, primed for interruption.

"Yes, why?"

"You're crying," he said.

I touched my eyes and found them wet and raw. "I don't remember doing that."

"What did you see?" he asked, glancing at Avery. "Did you find out what you wanted to know?"

"Yeah," I said with a nod. "I think I did. Just wasn't the answer I wanted."

"Come on. I'll signal Haden and Devin that we're leaving. Grim aside, I see what you mean about the crazy rubbing off. This place is loaded with enough painful memories even I can feel it. What do we do about her?" Priest glanced at the grim.

I couldn't help but think about the horrid things the husband had been doing to this body, but I had no sympathy for the grim. If it wanted to leave, it could. We, on the other hand, had a better chance of leaving if Avery was exactly as we found her. "No, we stand a better chance if she's intact."

Peanut Butter and Straight Jackets

W E STEPPED OUT INTO the hallway and called to the husband that we were done. I could hear the music downstairs, but I didn't hear footsteps coming to meet us. The music resonated an eerie, false cheerfulness. After a good minute wait, we headed downstairs without our escort. The bedrooms caught my eye again.

I couldn't imagine what pain this man had gone through in losing his whole family. I had lost my adoptive parents before the apocalypse, and I had no siblings. My parents' distant relations were not close to us, so I had only my friends to mourn. However, I could understand being alone. Every *apocagee* knew that feeling.

When we reached the main floor, the temptation to rip the board off the door by hand and run like hell was overwhelming. Priest must have sensed my cowardice, because he took my hand again.

"Well?" The husband stepped out of the kitchen with a knife in hand. I nearly jumped out of my skin from the start he gave me. The knife, albeit a butter knife, didn't do anything to relax my death grip on Priest's hand. "Is she one of God's chosen ones?"

"We must consult with our associates to confirm our beliefs," Priest said quickly, before I could say anything. The husband's face melted and he returned to the kitchen.

With no hammer to pry the door open, we followed him into the square, center-island kitchen. The boxed fluorescent lights made the tan cupboards look yellow. The husband was preparing a feast of mangled peanut butter and jelly sandwiches—none of which looked appealing, since his hands were filthy.

"If you wouldn't mind helping us with the door, sir. We can get the answers you seek," Priest said. I was impressed at his grace under pressure.

The man looked at Priest and then down at the cross I had made him. Though he often tucked it below his collar, to my knowledge he never took it off. I was concerned at one time he had traded his obsession with his collar for it, but I was certain now he wore it because I gave it to him. It was a sweet gesture, I thought, since it was hardly attractive.

"Father." Priest winced at the title. "Before you go, I need to confess my sins."

There was a moment of panic I couldn't hide from either of them. I wanted to get the hell out of there, but we had to continue playing the part. This man was too crazy to piss off, and without a hammer or a pry bar, we weren't leaving. It was best to keep the nut-job appeased.

"Certainly, my son," Priest said in a voice I imagined he used a lot with his parishioners. They left the kitchen and I heard the music in the dining room rise and fall as they entered and shut the door behind them.

With little time to spare—or perhaps a lot if the guy had been as naughty in real life as he was now—I ran out to the front room and pried against the board holding the door. As I suspected, I wouldn't be able to pry it off without a lever of some kind.

I ran back to the kitchen in search for something to use. I grabbed a chef's knife and ran back to the door. I wedged it under the edge of the board and worked the nails loose enough to get a finger hold. The knife wasn't going to get me any farther, so I tossed it noiselessly onto the carpet.

I heard the music rise again and I quickly unlocked the dead bolt and the knob. I turned around and tried to act as casual as one can while trying to escape the house of a lunatic. The husband eyed me warily as he shut the door behind him. I was as aware of Priest's absence as I was of the shotgun hanging by his thigh.

"What are you doing?" he asked, no doubt unconvinced of my innocence.

"Where's Priest?" I asked, ignoring his question.

"He's meditating."

For a moment, we both stared at each other, him with the eyes of a lonely deluded man, me with the eyes of someone who knew better than to feel sorry for him. Crazy people were the worst to go head to head with. The grim were evil and intended to do evil things, but the crackpots were tricky. One minute they were rational and lucid, the next... let's just say my biggest concern wasn't being shot.

"Priest!" I yelled loudly, breaking our unspoken pretense of civility.

"He can't hear you," the man said, his voice rolling low into what some considered to be a mid-western accent. To me it was just lazy pronunciation.

"What did you do to him?" I asked, taking a step forward. I should have taken a step back, but the thought of Priest lying behind the dining room door bleeding to death was making me antsy. I wish I could have called it bravery, but I was still thinking about running back to the door and taking my chances that the man would go after me rather than shoot me.

"He'll be alright. Just a nap."

I took that for "*I knocked him over the head with the butt of my gun,*" which relaxed me a little, even though I couldn't trust he was telling the truth. "What do you want?" I asked, falling deep into the muddy waters of psychopath banter.

He stepped to the side, forcing me to shift away from the door to keep my distance. He was smarter than I had given him credit for. "It's been a lonely couple of years," he said with enough honesty that I might have sympathized if the madness wasn't dripping off him like the Mad Hatter. "It's so hard being on my own."

"You're not on your own. You have Avery," I reminded him cheerfully, steering my way to the dining room door.

He grimaced at the sound of her name. "I've had about as much fun as I can have with her. She should have stayed dead. Can't trust her any more now than when she was alive."

I felt myself tense with the realization that he knew Avery had died. This guy wasn't one of your run-of-the-mill denial cases. He kept Avery around like a pet and playmate. A playmate he had grown tired of. Fortunately for him, I had arrived: young, female, alive. He would save a fortune on lubricant.

I threw myself at the dining room door. Somehow I managed to get the door open, shut, and locked before the husband moved. He either wasn't quick, or he wasn't concerned since I still didn't have an exit. Great, just what I needed—a rapist who liked a long chase.

"Priest!" I hissed in the dark room over the music that was starting to drive *me* crazy. "Priest!" I ran around the eight-chaired cherry wood table that was polished to a sickening sheen. Priest was laid out on the floor. Blood spilled out of his forehead. "Shit!"

I pressed my hands to his head. I felt for his heart rate and breathing. He was alive, but I couldn't wake him. He was going to be out longer than I could stall. I heard a thumping sound and looked up over the table.

I hadn't observed carefully enough. There was a swinging door from the kitchen. It thrummed into place with my favorite shot-gun-toting antihero on my side of it.

He danced around the table with me before attempting to leap over the top of it. He reached for me and snagged my shirt. I squealed in the way every ten-year-old girl does when they're scared. Unlike a ten-year-old girl, though, I followed up with a nose-breaking punch.

He released me to cradle his nose, and I booked it through the swinging doors. I calculated correctly that the door was still not an option, since he was likely to shoot me rather than lose me. Necrophilia was obviously not beneath him.

Instead, I headed upstairs to signal Haden and Devin. They should have been storming the place in another few minutes any-way, but that was a few minutes too late.

The doorknob shot off the dining room door as I passed. I dove against the stairs before scrambling up them in what seemed like slow motion.

His hand grabbed my ankle and I shrieked again. I could feel the images of his memories coming through me, but I was too scared to process them. Somehow, I pushed them aside, like a magazine article I could read later in the bathroom when I wasn't busy.

He started to climb up to reach the rest of me, but I kicked him in the crotch. Once again, he let me go to cradle his injured body, and I scrambled further up the steps. I heard his gun barrel rattle as he positioned it for his second shot. I flipped over in time to kick the muzzle up. The spray of pellets missed me by one step. I could smell the singed plastic carpet above me.

He cussed and started to reload, but I didn't wait for him to finish. He didn't bother rushing to follow me. After all, up the stairs was still not an escape route. I hate slow predators.

At the very least, I had time to signal for help. I ran back to the master bedroom, past the growling grim, to the window. I waved frantically at Devin and Haden, who were a couple hundred yards away to remain obscure. They were arguing about something and not paying attention to the window.

I tried to open the window, but unsurprisingly it was nailed shut. I heard footsteps on the stairs and I panicked. Dead was one thing, but being chained up in this guy's basement to be used as a playmate was another entirely.

I gave the cheap decorative post at the head of the bed a roundhouse kick and knocked the wood from its base. The grim snarled at me, but grinned with a madness that matched her caretaker. She seemed to understand my plan, and waited for me to come around and fracture the other post, effectively freeing her.

I was pinned between the dresser and the grim as she maneuvered herself free of the remaining structure. The husband flew in prepared to take me captive. The grim looked over us both and decided she would have more fun with him and lunged at him. He tried to run out and shut the door behind him, but the grim used a piece of the bed still dragging from her restraints to jam it. She ripped open the door and pursued him.

Once they were gone, I grabbed the other bedpost that had dropped at my feet. I hopped over the bed and rammed it through a pane of the window. After a second hit to break the environmentally preferred double-paned glass, I threw the post out onto the roof eve where it skittered and dropped to the ground below.

Thankfully, that was enough to draw back Devin's attention. He looked through his binoculars and I waved frantically. To my great relief he started running toward the house. I breathed in a few consoling breaths and ruminated on the idea that my hero was coming to rescue me.

It was in that moment my mind chose to bring out the magazine article I was supposed to read.

Once a Upon a Time

ONCE UPON A TIME would never be an appropriate beginning to a story with such malice, but nevertheless, this story did start out as a fairytale, as often nightmare relationships do. It was perhaps typical of an abusive relationship in that Avery had no idea how controlling and vicious Grady could be. One moment he was a loving husband of twin boys and a brand new baby girl, but then something changed.

Grady started to suggest the baby didn't look like him. The only rationale in his warped mind, of course, was that the child was blond, an aberration from the dark hair of her parents. Not understanding the complexity of recessive genes, he persisted to interrogate Avery about her fidelity.

Avery denied the accusations whole-heartedly, but Grady was not convinced. Long before she was ever a grim, he tied her to the bed and starved her of nearly every drop of food until she wasted away. Without her mother to breastfeed, and no formula offered, the infant died long before anyone else.

Grady cut her hair, insisting she would no longer be attractive to men, therefore could not cheat on him again. Avery pleaded her innocence and begged for release, even as he took his marital liberties with her. She beseeched him for the sake of her twin boys, who were too young to run away from the house of terror, but too old not to understand that their father was a very bad man.

The boys, not fully six, learned to pick the lock on their mother's door so they could sneak in to see her. It was the only joy left in her captive life. By then she knew her baby was dead, just as she knew Grady would eventually kill her.

Months into her captivity, Grady caught the boys on one such visit. He gently goaded the children back to their beds and read them a story. As they drifted off to sleep, Grady watched them. When they were asleep, he raised the shotgun to their chests one at a time.

My Heroes

HEARING THE REAL SHOTGUN blast downstairs jerked me from Grady's memories. My eyes were wet with tears again, but I felt angry more than sad. I stomped out of the master bedroom and into the twins' room to see for myself.

I stopped between the beds and pulled back the covers. Beneath the layers of quilts were two ruined torsos lying on bloodstained sheets. I hissed and threw the blankets back over them.

I had never been so irate. I was appalled a man could be capable of this, but I was furious I had been put in the same lot as him and kept on Earth. I was beginning to understand the condescension Priest felt for all of us so-called non-believers.

I heard Grady's feet gallop up the stairs in search of me. I tucked myself behind the door. He went to the master bedroom where he had last seen me. I was emotional enough to attempt an attack, but he still had one shot left in his gun, and I couldn't risk a close-up fight with a shotgun.

Instead, I tiptoed around the door and ran down the stairs. I was at the bottom when I heard the shot. I was pushed forward by tiny hot coals burrowing into my back. I crashed into the floor, struggling to breathe. I cried out, but realized there was no one around to help me, so I stopped.

I struggled to remember what I knew about shotguns. I knew that at some distance you could shoot a person and not even break the skin. I, however, was not within that category, but if the bullets hadn't severed my spine, or lacerated any vital organs, I might still live. Might, except Grady was reloading.

I bit my lip and sucked in a breath that hurt like hell. I pushed with my feet—which I was happy weren't paralyzed—and I pulled with my hands. I dragged a bloody trail across the carpet in my effort to get to the door. Then I heard Devin shouting my name outside.

I hollered back to him as best I could and his efforts to get in doubled. Grady joined me on the main floor, but instead of pointing his gun at me, he aimed it at the door. Devin only needed one more good push against the nailed board and he would be in. He would arrive in time for the same treatment I just got, but at closer range.

With only seconds to think, I remembered the knife I had used to pry up the wood. I rolled over despite the pressure on my wounds being pure agony. I found the knife to my right, grabbed the hilt and threw it. All too late, I realized I should have grabbed the blade.

The hilt bounced off Grady's face, but it was enough to disrupt his aim. Devin crashed through the door, nearly falling to the floor. Haden followed with her gun in hand. She was firing before I saw her face. Three bullets downed Grady, though one shot from Haden would have killed him.

Devin was at my side, prepared to scoop me up and run with me. "No," I rasped, feeling the pressure of the floor against my wounds. "Get Priest, he's in there." I pointed vaguely to the dining room, and Devin didn't hesitate to see what further damage needed to be undone.

Haden took his place beside me, manhandling me as only she could. She rolled me back onto my stomach and ripped my shirt open to see my back. "My lungs hurt. I can't get a good breath," I informed her.

"Any blood in your mouth?" she asked without any hint of concern; just taking inventory.

"No," I said and she leaned back away from me. "Am I going to die?" Haden would certainly tell me the truth. I hadn't considered it an option with the armed loon running around, but now that he was dead, I was prepared to lie back and give my croaked goodbyes.

"No," Haden said, almost disgusted that I was being overdramatic. "But you definitely need a dentist."

Lidocaine and Bullets

As a general rule, there weren't a lot of doctors left post apocalypse—or lawyers, for that matter. Most people attributed it to the services they provided. Somehow, their sins were balanced out by their humanitarian efforts. I for one had my own school of thought: God was fucking with us to make this apocalypse even harder, but that was hardly good dinner conversation.

At some point, the pain of being lugged around like a sack of potatoes knocked me out. I was grateful to reawaken already face down in the dentist chair. The headrest had been shifted to provide me a chin rest, and I was lying as flat as the chair allowed.

"She's awake." Devin crouched down into my line of sight. "He's about to start injecting."

I turned my head back to peek at the elderly lavender-gray-haired man with magnifying glasses. He looked like a mad scientist, but beggars can't be choosers—certainly not when the beggar has birdshot in her back.

The long needle he held jetted out a stream of liquid before he directed it at my back. I pinched my eyes shut and braced for the torture, but I was already up to the frowny face on my pain chart. The stinging sensation of the injections were mere tickles compared to the pain I already had from the bullet pellets.

"Where's Priest?" I asked when I realized my pain was only lessening with each shot.

"I'm here," he said from somewhere behind me. Devin gave him a gesture to invite him over, followed by wide eyes of demand when he didn't immediately come forward. Priest stepped into my view and kneeled before me. He looked guilty. He must have blamed himself for the whole fiasco, since he was the one who convinced everyone to let me do it.

"Are you okay?" I asked, scanning the cut over his left eye.

He smiled and glanced at Devin before touching my cheek lightly. "Lenore, you've been shot in the back. How can you be worried about me?"

"Because I already know what's wrong with me." I frowned. "I'm sorry. I didn't mean to get you hurt."

"You?" He looked down and shook his head. When he looked back up, whatever he was going to say had changed. "I hope you got the information you wanted. Devin isn't likely to approve another field trip any time soon," he murmured and glanced to wherever Devin had moved to.

I thought back to my conversation with the grim. Everything was vague, but I now knew what I had suspected all along, but couldn't quite verbalize. The grim were just a nuisance and not the main threat against us. That honor was held by Adrian Dorn and his ilk. Unfortunately, I still didn't know what his ultimate goal was. Apparently, it was too much to hope for an open and honest bad guy.

"I did," I said and whimpered as I felt something cold digging into my back. I glanced back and saw Haden playing nurse for the doctor. She was holding a tray of variously shaped silver pliers. I assumed they were designed to pull teeth, but tooth or pellet, extraction was still the ultimate goal.

The sight of the bloodied tips made my head go foggy and my stomach roil. "I think I'm going to puke."

"Just rest, Lenore." Priest touched my cheek again, and I felt the warmth. This time, however, it was as if Snuggles was giving me a bear hug. I couldn't fight the desire to lay my head down and sleep.

Chicken Soup for
Broken Soul Mates

WHEN I WOKE, I was home. I was in August's old room. It was considered the master bedroom even though it wasn't very big, but it did have twin closets. I was lying on her queen bed face down, covered in what was possibly the heaviest quilt ever made. Whoever lived in this house pre-apocalypse had a very tenacious grandmother.

I could see the sun was setting outside. I wasn't sure if it was the night of or the night after my injuries, but either way I hurt and I had to pee. I maneuvered my way out of bed and used the restroom. On my way back, I saw Priest coming upstairs with a tray of food. He took one look at me moving around and his eyes went cartoon buggy.

"What are you doing? You're going to start bleeding again."

"I had to pee," I defended myself.

"Get back in bed before Devin sees you," he hissed.

I understood Devin would be concerned for my health, but I was a little surprised Priest was prioritizing Devin's composure. Rather than argue, I scurried back into August's room and sat on the bed. I wasn't ready to get back under the covers. Lying on my back wasn't an option, and I certainly couldn't eat what Priest had brought me if I was face down.

"What did you bring me?" I asked after he shut the door part way with his foot.

He furrowed his brow and looked at the tray. "This is my dinner."

"Oh," I said, thoroughly disappointed and suddenly ravenous.

He smiled at me and laughed. "Lenore, of course it's for you." I smiled, pretending my brain wasn't about to start bleaching my roots. "How are you feeling?" he asked as he sat down on the bed, putting the tray between us.

I resisted the urge to say fine, because I wasn't. Instead I shrugged, which made me groan with pain. "Oh crap, I can't believe I just did that." Priest reached his hand to touch my cheek, and I pulled away. "Don't, don't put me to sleep."

He sighed and retracted his hand. "I wasn't. I was going to take some of your pain."

"Then you'll be in pain," I rebuked him.

"Rightfully so," he mumbled, grabbing a white oval pill from the tray. "Here then, this is the good stuff."

"What do you mean, rightfully so?" I asked, taking the pill in hand, but not swallowing it. I was more interested in the grilled cheese sandwich and tomato soup anyway.

"Nothing." Priest shook his head. "Here, eat something—"

"Bullshit. What happened after I passed out?"

"Devin..." He paused, grinding his teeth. "He blames me for what happened."

"You were knocked out."

"I got caught up in playing the part of the priest. I let my guard down. It shouldn't have happened. I shouldn't have left you alone. I shouldn't have turned my back on that bastard."

"It's not your fault. I wanted to go there. I wouldn't have gotten in without you."

"I can't protect you like he would!" Priest stood and walked to the window and stared out at the sunset like it was the cause of his irritation.

I knew Devin would have blamed anyone for my mistakes except me, but that wasn't the reason Priest was taking it to heart. Something else was bothering him. Something to do with my recent break up, if I was understanding correctly which "he" he was referring to.

I stood and joined him at the window, but I didn't speak. I wasn't necessarily waiting for him to speak. I just didn't know what to say.

"I hated seeing you with him," he said, breaking the silence before me. "He was necessary, I know. I shouldn't have been jealous. I practically pushed you to him." I wanted to tell him that he *did* push me to him, but I held my tongue. "I was glad you sent him away, but after tonight, I'm wondering if it wasn't premature."

"Funny, I was thinking it was long overdue."

He turned to face me. "Why did you send him away? I mean, why now?"

I took in a deep breath, which hurt, but I turned my grimace into feigned contemplation so Priest wouldn't fret about it. "After the visit from the Seraphim, I couldn't help but think about how many creatures might be trying to get a foothold on the Earth, or on us. I know everyone's been telling me that there's a war coming, but I guess I didn't take it seriously until then. I've never been particularly worried about the grim, but territorial angels...

"Somehow, bickering with Garrett about our relationship problems seemed so infantile. I only stayed with him out of loneliness, then it was convenience, and then it was just out of pity. He's a good man, and I really do hope he can mend things with his wife, but his exit was long overdue. The only reason he was staying with me, was to avoid her and his loss. When I found out about her, he clung to me even tighter, like he was afraid if he lost me, he would be instantly transported back to the reality of his life without his children."

Priest nodded like a few details in my uncharacteristic morality shift were falling into place. He didn't pry too much about Garrett's marital status, but I knew he was annoyed I had persisted to be with a married man, even though the boundaries of monogamy had pretty much gone to hell.

"Still," he said, looking contemplative, "Garrett is far more prepared for situations like yesterday."

"No one could be prepared for that asshole. Don't pretend like you are completely useless. You've helped me out plenty of times."

"I've got a good parlor trick for the grim, but I'm afraid it's not enough. I can't protect you, not the way I was hoping." He looked away.

"I never expected you to be a warrior and I'm not defenseless," I said.

He turned back to me, enunciating his words so I understood his particular version of the English language. "If I can't protect you, I'm a liability."

"You can knock grim out with a single touch. How is a liability?"

His eyes darted over mine as if I was telling him something he didn't know already. "We aren't just fighting grim though, are we?" He motioned to world outside the window. "We're fighting angels and demons and every other underrepresented creature of the Bible."

"Who better to fight them than a priest?"

"All I have is what God has lent me. I'm not sure it's enough for what's coming, but you have something else." I rolled my eyes. "Listen to me!" His voice cut my attitude like a knife and I resisted the urge to step away from him. "I know you're sick of hearing this, but you *are* special. August didn't stumble onto you. She was searching for you. There's something inside you, something powerful. I felt it that day when you fought against my mind and I felt it again when you were reading the grim. You just need to take the blinders off and see it."

I gave in to my urge to step away, but Priest grabbed me and pulled me back. Unprepared to catch myself, I fell against his chest, and to my surprise he wrapped me loosely in his arms. There was a twinge of pain, but I ignored it, focusing on his chest pressing against mine. My lips parted under the pretense of talking or breathing, but really, I was begging him to kiss me.

To my dismay and aggravation, he didn't. He continued to speak. "You are extraordinary and exquisite. Even under the influence of drugs and alcohol, I saw that in you from the very first time we met. I'm drawn to you, Lenore, just like August was, but I am not helping you right now. I hope someday I can, but until then, I need to get out of your way."

"What?" I pulled away from him, recreating the distance I wanted moments earlier. "Out of my way? What are you saying?"

Priest swallowed hard before speaking softly, as if my heart was a soufflé about to fall. "I'm saying that I'm going to leave... for a while."

I shook my head, letting my mouth fall open for a moment. "Are you freaking kidding me?" I yelled.

I couldn't believe what I was hearing. I had finally gotten the nerve to dump Garrett and focus on my defense of the world. In an effort to gather up information for just such a task, I had been shot in the back. Now, even before I had begun to heal, the man I love, who supposedly loved me, was leaving me, *again*.

"Lenore I know this sounds cruel and ill-timed, but I need to sort out a few things. I thought I knew what my purpose here was, but I was wrong."

I knew exactly how this conversation was supposed to go. He was going to rationalize his abandonment so I would be calm enough to see him out the door instead of throwing breakables at him, like I wanted to. However, I wasn't going to play by the rules.

"Get out!"

"What?" It was his turn to be shocked into inquiry.

"You heard me. Get your shit, and get out!"

"Lenore, I'm not leaving you forever," he pleaded.

"Don't you even start with me, you selfish son of a bitch. You have been dangling your love for me like a damned carrot just out of reach for the last few months. It doesn't matter if you're here or not here. Liability, you are not, but a pain in my ass, you are! I'm so sick of men doling out an allotment of themselves to me like I'm not worthy of a whole pie. I can have Devin anytime I want, but I have to share him with Haden. I can have Garrett, but only the sorrowful, guilty part, because the loving, charismatic part belongs to his wife. And you! Well forget that, because you're in a perpetual relationship loop with God. Maybe this time he'll take you back—nope, maybe this time, or this time."

Priest narrowed his eyes at my humor.

"Here's my new philosophy: men are philandering, cheating, lying bastards, which, by the way, is what I thought of all of you before the end of the world, so I guess it's not a new philosophy as much as an old one dusted off. At any rate, fuck you, get out of my house, and don't bother coming back this time, because your exit is a little overdue too!"

Priest stared at me a moment longer, possibly debating on arguing, or perhaps he wanted to see if my conviction would waver. It didn't. He gathered up the few things he had brought into the bedroom, and headed out. There was a very short conversation downstairs followed by the slamming of the front side door.

I refused to watch his vehicle pull away. Instead, I went back to the bed and ate my grilled cheese sandwich and willed myself not to cry. I managed to make it to the soup before I finally broke down into sobs. A little extra salt in the soup made no difference.

Missing Pieces

I T TOOK A GOOD week before I got back to some semblance of normal. Devin had pampered me too much, and to balance my ego, Haden offered me no sympathy whatsoever. In that sense, things were back to normal.

Devin started to flirt with me more freely, since he was no longer concerned with trespassing on Garrett's territory. Meanwhile, Haden was terse, as always.

For the first time, though, I felt August's vacancy. After the funeral, Garrett and Priest were there. Now that they were gone, I was painfully aware of the number three.

As I sat on the couch reading, a half thought kept popping into my head. Something had been bothering me since my incident with Grady. I had practically lived the entire horrific incident through his eyes. I knew how his children had died.

They hadn't died at the apocalypse. They had died just before it. They died as flesh and blood, yet they clearly had crystallized tissues. How? Why?

I had seen enough suicide victims to know the people who died post-apocalypse were not offered such a privilege. What about people who died before the rapture? Were tickets to the gates of heaven offered posthumously? If so, wouldn't cemeteries be dispelling bodies, left and right, or were they immune to the surfacing by some Lazarus clause?

The bodies the Seraphim were using were already decomposed. None of them had been crystallized, so perhaps it had more to do with the proximity to the event. Perhaps the crystallization was a small blessing offered to us by God so we didn't have to deal with the stench and disease of a genocidal amount of rotting corpses. If so, I really needed to send a thank you card.

That thought process led me to another loose-ended detail. I remembered Priest coming home that night inexplicably muddy after an unannounced evening out. At the time, it was strange, but now it seemed suspect. The more I thought about it, the more I started to piece together that half a thought into a whole one.

***

The cemetery was dark, but I positioned the four-wheeler with the lights roughly in the direction I was heading. It only served to cast tall shadows beyond the first two rows of stones, but I could see my feet enough not to step into an open grave—which, let's face it, is really the biggest concern about walking in a graveyard at night.

I weaved through epitaphs for people I didn't know and never would. At best, they might have been familiar strangers if I had known them alive. I still dreaded the day when I would come across a familiar grim. So far, I couldn't call any of them by name.

When I reached August's gravesite, I tripped over something and landed on the grass of someone else's plot. Pardoning myself, I looked over August's place of rest. I did a double take on the nameplate to make sure I had the right person. It was her grave, but the soil was freshly turned and slightly mounded over the plot, as if she had been buried yesterday.

I bit back a yelp when I saw what I had tripped on: A portion of the body bag we had buried August in was poking through the dirt at the base of the plot. I shuddered and forced myself to look further. I wiped away the dirt at the head of the mound. When I touched plastic just underneath the soil, I withdrew my hand.

It took every ounce of bravery I had to fight against the creepiness of darkness, bugs, and things that go bump. I pushed more dirt away, revealing the zipper at the top of the body bag. Slowly I unzipped it, and unveiled August's face.

My magnanimous heroine was still beautiful. Not a bit of her had changed, except that her perfect glowing skin was now sandy like a beach. She had joined the ranks of the crystalline dead. Somehow, post-apocalypse, she had won favor with God. Until now, I hadn't even known that was possible. I just assumed we were all going to hell.

Priest and Garrett had hidden this from me, and perhaps even the others. I should have been mad, but I knew why they had done it. Priest knew I was uncomfortable with the duties that had been set on my shoulders. He knew if I fully understood my importance, it would scare me.

The real dirty secret was not August rising from her grave. It wasn't even that there was a chance to reconcile with God. The secret he didn't want me to know was that the goal August had strived to achieve: her search for me, her plan to fight the evil coming down on the Earth. All of it was for Him. She had been acting on His behalf and now I, the antithesis to organized religion and formulaic faith, was supposed to take her place.

God help us all.

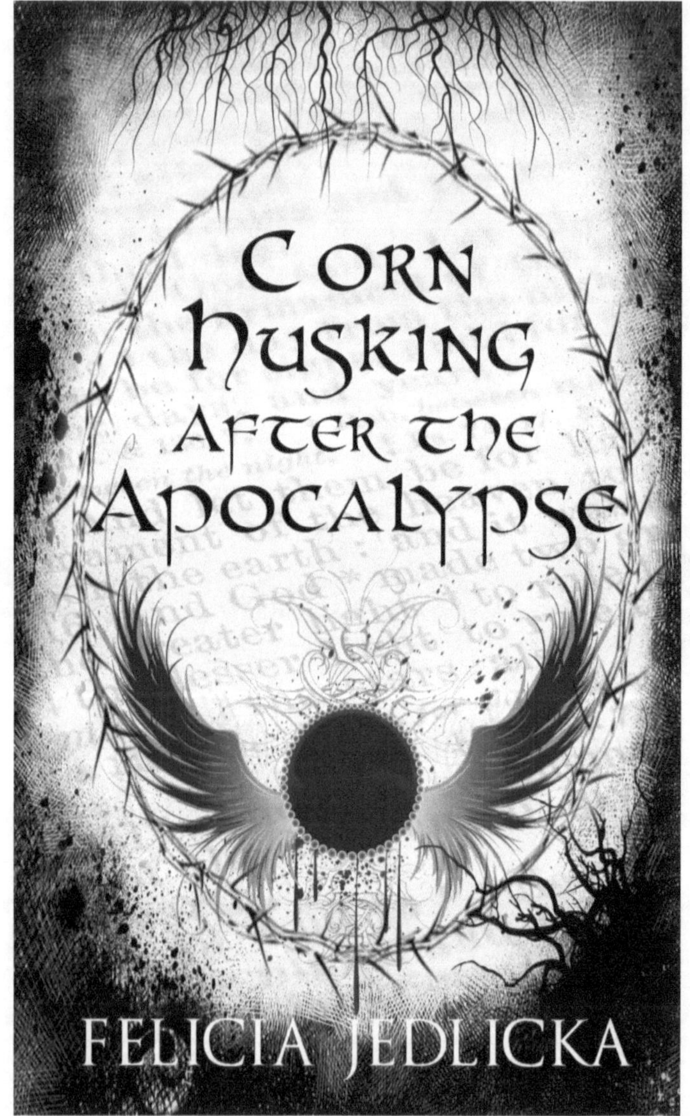

CORN
HUSKING
AFTER THE
APOCALYPSE

FELICIA JEDLICKA

Corn Husking After the Apocalypse

Book 3 of the Nebraska Apocalypse Novels

WITH MORE THAN ENOUGH devils to go around, the survivors of the reckoning are finding dangers lurking around every corner. If it's not the demon-ridden dead, it's the remainder of the human population that's gone from crazy to feral.

The impending war is looming in Lenore's every waking thought, and her arch-nemesis is poisoning her dreams with psychosexual torture. What little enthusiasm she has left for heroes' work is quickly being depleted. With the future of humanity at stake, she must endure and resist the temptation to surrender.

About the Author

As a Nebraska native, and a small-town girl at that, I have very little to occupy my time beyond imagining a world outside of my own reality. By the grace of God and the seat of my pants, I have kept my waning attention span on the task of becoming an author.

So here I am, an indie author, peddling my words in cyberspace and enduring my comeuppances with an unwavering determination. I may not be a professional, and I certainly am not perfect, but if you've made it this far, you have to admit, this smartass yokel does spin quite a yarn.

From the self-inflicted sweatshop conditions of my unairconditioned childhood home, to the arthritis reaping positions of a sedentary lifestyle, I bring to you: my sarcasm, my oddity, and my heart. Take it with a grain of salt or a teaspoon of sugar, but take it for what it is: a story born of the mind, translated to paper, and gifted to you.

I thank you for your readership and even more for your support.